Promises

Kimberly Lyons

Mary,
Hope you enjoy
this
Kimberly C Lyons

Lyons Den Publishing
St. Clair Shores, MI 48080
1998

PROMISES

Published by:
Lyons Den Publishing
24313 Harmon, St Clair Shores MI 48080

ISBN 0-9666027-0-6

 All characters in this book are fictitious, not based on any person living or dead.

Printed in the United States by:
Morris Publishing, 3212 East Highway 30, Kearney, NE 68847

To all those who helped in this endeavor, I give many thanks, especially to Denise, for all the encouragement you've given me, and to my wonderful husband, Alan. Without your inspiration I doubt any of this would have been possible.

I dedicate this book to my mom, who is no longer with me in body, but always in spirit. I wish I had finished this while you were still alive, Mom.

(And Dad--Thanks)

My comfort in my sufferings is this:
Your promise renews my life.
Psalm 119:50

Prologue

The boy knew he wasn't supposed to be playing by the ridge. His mother had told him so many times how dangerous it was to play near there. But the big boys had kicked him out of the school yard, and there was no where else to play. The town was small, and heaven knew there was no one with a great deal of money, which meant the houses were small with only tiny yards in which to play. That's what led Benny to the ridge. He wanted room to play.

Now he was in serious trouble. His ball had fallen over the edge of the ridge, and being the boy he was, he went after it, instead of just leaving it there and getting a new one. Not that his mom could afford another one. This was the fourth ball he had lost since Halloween. Now it was almost Thanksgiving, and his mom wouldn't be happy about his losing another ball. So he had scrambled down the rocky ridge to the ledge where his ball rested in a scraggly bush. The rocks were icy, and it was very difficult to keep his balance. He grabbed the wayward ball, but when he tried to climb back up, it was too slippery.

He started to cry. If only he had listened to his mom. She was constantly reminding him to listen and obey, but he usually did what he wanted anyway. He guessed that was the reason most adults blamed him when something went wrong. Now, because of his disobedience, he was stuck there on the ridge, with his grip slipping quickly. It was getting harder and harder to hold on.

He started yelling at the top of his voice. "Help! Help!" he cried. But it was no use. There was no one around to help him. His hand had almost slipped off the rock he was clutching when another, larger hand, covered it. Benny looked up into the warm brown eyes of Pastor Williams, the minister at his church.

Just relax, Benny,"his soothing voice floated calmly down to the boy.

Benny's tears slowly dried as the man came the rest of the way down to the narrow ledge where Benny was standing. There wasn't much room to spare, but Benny figured Pastor Williams knew what he was doing.

"I'm going to push you up to the top, Benny, O.K.?" Benny looked up, gray eyes filled with terror. "Don't worry. I won't let you fall. But you have to promise me not to ever play here again. Is that a promise?"

"Yes, sir," Benny whispered. "I promise to do whatever you say."

Pastor Williams glanced down to the river flowing below, knowing it hid a multitude of rocks and boulders. He had a strange feeling of closure, as if he wasn't going to return to the top of the ridge himself. He said a silent prayer. *Is this it, Lord?* He remained quiet, and felt the Lord speaking to his heart. He closed his eyes, readying himself for what was to come.

"Benny?"

"Yes, sir?" the boy answered, his voice trembling.

"There is one more promise I'd like you to make," Pastor Williams said.

"O.K."

"Promise me that you'll take my place."

"What do you mean, Pastor Williams? I can't do that. I'm just a kid. And a bad kid too," Benny whispered brokenly.

"Look at me, Benny," the Pastor commanded. When Benny's tear-filled gray eyes met warm brown ones, Pastor Williams continued. "You are not a bad boy, Benny. You just need to remember that Jesus died for you, and try to be like Him. He loves you so much. He wants you to love Him with all your heart. If you put Him first in your life you won't be 'bad' any more. Do you want to do that Benny?" the Pastor asked.

"I don't know if I can, Pastor Williams. I love Jesus, but every time I do something it turns out bad. And I can't seem to help but do the wrong thing." Benny's tears started falling again.

Pastor Williams looked down at the boy, love lighting his brown eyes. He had always had a soft spot for this little boy with no father to guide him. "Let Jesus shine in your heart, Benny. I know He's there. I see it every time I see you with your mom. You treat her like she's the most important person in the world."

"She is," Benny interrupted. "I'd do anything for her. But I disobeyed," Benny cried. "She'll hate me now."

"Oh, Benny, she could never hate you. She loves you like Jesus does. Now, I'm going to push you up so you can go tell her how much you love her, and that you will do your best not to disobey again, O.K.?"

"O.K., Pastor Williams."

"And Benny?"

"Yes, sir?"

"Remember that I love you, too." Benny gave the Pastor a watery smile, then felt Pastor Williams' hands pushing him up to the top of the ridge.

When Benny finally managed to pull himself the rest of the way, he was exhausted. He turned around to thank Pastor Williams, but the man wasn't there. Benny looked over the side to see Pastor Williams desperately grasping a flimsy branch sticking out of the wall of the cliff. "I'll go get help!" Benny cried. But before he could leave Pastor Williams' voice stopped him.

"Don't worry Benny. Just remember how much Jesus loves you. And remember, you promised to do whatever I asked." The man tried pulling himself up, but just as he got a grip on the top, his foot slipped on the icy rocks and he fell into the ravine below.

Benny watched in horror as his rescuer hit the icy water and rocks below. "No!" he screamed. But it was too late. Tears streamed down his face. Pastor Williams was the only person other than his mom who had ever loved him and now he was gone.

He was sitting, curled up in a small ball, and crying when the first people arrived at the ridge. They had seen the man fall, and came rushing to the scene. They found Benny sitting at the edge, sobbing. They tried to question him, but the boy was too distraught to answer. The police arrived shortly thereafter, and pieced together what had happened.

The next few days were the worst Benny had ever lived through. Even though the police determined it was an accident, he knew most of the people blamed him for Pastor Williams' death. He might only have been ten years old, but he understood what those looks meant. That awful boy, those looks said, look what he did to that wonderful man.

Benny never said a word. Before this had happened, he probably would have sassed back to anyone whose eyes accused him. Now he remembered Pastor Williams' words. He had to put his hurt and anger behind him and accept the blame for the accident. He tried hard to go on with his life, but it was difficult. It seemed as if a day didn't go by that one of his schoolmates would murmur under their breath about the boy who had killed the preacher. It became so bad his mom finally sat him down in their little house to tell him she was sending him to live with his grandparents in Montana.

"I don't want to go, Ma," Benny cried. "Please don't send me away. I didn't mean to kill Pastor Williams. I didn't."His tears fell freely.

Benny's mother gathered him close. "You didn't kill anyone, sweetheart. It was an accident. But I can tell you're hurting, and staying here is only going to hurt you more. I can't go with you. It would be too hard for me to get another job. But your Gramma and Grampa said that they would love to have you come live on the ranch for awhile. And as much as I will miss you, I think it would be for the best. I will not let these people hurt you anymore," her voice was hard and determined.

So when the Christmas holiday came, Benny went to live in Montana with his grandparents. But he never forgot Pastor Williams' last words to him.

One

Arianna Jenkins stood looking over the town from the crest of the hill. From this vantage point everything looked so beautiful, so peaceful. Even from half a mile away, the hill offered a wonderful view of the town and its inhabitants. The river tumbling merrily through the town square, an offshoot of the one raging behind her, was clearly visible, its blue-green waters sparkling in the sun. Anna could see the residents of Jordon going through their daily routines, the same ones she had been watching for the past three weeks.

Anna let out a long sigh. When she arrived in Jordon three weeks ago, it was with the conviction that it would only be a temporary situation, a few weeks at most. She may have promised her dying mother she would visit the woman's hometown, but she never said anything about staying for any length of time. After all, Anna was a born and bred 'city-girl'.

But in the three weeks she had been there, Anna had lost her heart to the beautiful, peaceful little town. It wasn't that she didn't like where she had been living. She enjoyed her life in Southern California. The list of things to do was endless, and she had many friends to keep her occupied. But when her mom had fallen ill, Anna learned a great deal about what was really important in life.

Jackie Jenkins meant the world to her daughter. They had been alone together since Anna was a baby. Anna had always believed her father had died soon after she was born, but during her mother's illness Anna learned her father had left them to seek fame and fortune, telling his wife that a family wasn't what he had in mind. He was killed in a barroom brawl shortly after Anna had turned four. Although the news had shocked Anna, she was thankful for her mother's honesty, if not her timing. It also made Anna realize why her mother had made such a fuss when Anna recently began dating an actor.

"That was your father's dream," Jackie told her daughter. "He wanted to be a big star. Unfortunately, he put his dreams ahead of his wife and daughter." The words sounded bitter, but Anna knew better. Jackie made it clear that she still loved Anna's father despite his lack of commitment to her and their child, and believed that one day he would have returned.

Anna did not share those beliefs. Her recent past showed her first hand how selfish desire could change a person. When she first began dating Lance Creel, Anna was flattered that someone as handsome and famous as he would even notice her. Although she had been told she was quite beautiful, she never considered herself to be. Her hair was a deep auburn, almost the color of a copper penny, and waved thick and soft down her back, almost to her waist. Most people exclaimed about how lovely it was. Most times she considered it an encumbrance, something to be shoved out of her eyes too often. Her eyes were a dark, dark brown, fringed with naturally long lashes. Anna had always wanted green eyes, so tended to ignore the compliments she received about their amazing depth.

Lance had seen Anna at a party and wasted no time in finding someone to introduce them. Luckily for him, a mutual acquaintance reluctantly did the honors, and Lance immediately asked for a date. Anna, attracted to Lance's rakish good looks, didn't hesitate in saying yes. At first he was the perfect gentleman. But it was soon obvious that Lance was less than a gentleman. Not a date went by that he didn't try to persuade Anna to go to bed with him. She always refused, gently telling him she intended to wait until she was married. At first he accepted her refusals gracefully, but as each date passed he became more and more insistent with the demand.

Shortly after the last awful confrontation, Anna's mother had become ill, and Anna had dropped everything to return home and nurse her ailing mother. Needless to say, Lance was not pleased, but could do nothing since he was working on location, having received a part in a major motion picture.

"We'll talk when I get back," he declared, during one of his few phone calls to her.

Anna had been happy to put off the inevitable. She knew she had to tell Lance their relationship was over, but was thankful she would have a few months respite before having to face that prospect. She then spent several happy weeks with her mother.

At least they had been happy until Jackie had coerced Anna into promising to visit Jackie's hometown after her death. "Why, Mama? We have never been back there, ever. There's no one left. Why do you want me to go?" Anna protested. She did not want to return to a town her mother had left so long ago.

"Because I want you to, Arianna," was the only answer her mother would give. Anna loved her mother very much, and since she believed her mother would be alive for a long time to come, she finally capitulated. The shock of Jackie's death the next day had stunned Anna. How could she be gone so quickly? Anna wondered sadly. With her promise to her mother uppermost in her mind, Anna sorrowfully made arrangements for her mother's funeral and for her own trip to Jordon, Virginia.

Anna sighed heavily as she pushed the memories from her mind. She had fallen in love with the town in the first week she had been there, and was even more enchanted with it after three weeks. It was quiet and cozy, with friendly people who actually spoke to you on the street. It was a town she realized she could live happily in, and she was seriously thinking of moving to Jordon permanently.

Her sigh turned to a groan of frustration. There were to many questions with no answers. Pushing her hair away from her face, she began walking down the hill. Her problematic relationship with Lance was only one cloud on her horizon, although in her opinion it was like a huge thundercloud compared to anything else. In the month since her mother's funeral he had never once tried to contact her. She had checked her answering machine, but there were no messages, either. After several calls to his agent, she had finally been told that Lance was still on location and wasn't likely to be back for at least another month. She left her phone number in Jordon with the agent, also leaving it on Lance's answering machine, hoping he would call, yet afraid he might. Anna wasn't one who liked leaving loose ends, and her relationship with Lance was definitely dangling over her head. But after their last encounter she was nervous about talking with him.

Wrapped up in her own thoughts, Anna didn't notice there was someone walking up the hill until she ran full tilt into him. With a soft 'umph' she collided with a man who seemed, at least to her soft body, as solid as a rock. She would have fallen if he had not reached out and caught her.

"Excuse me," Anna murmured, looking up into somber gray eyes.

"I didn't hurt you, did I?" the man questioned gently, steadying her before he let her go.

Anna took a breath before answering. She wasn't hurt, just terribly embarrassed. Her arms tingled where the man had held her. "No, I'm fine," she assured him.

He smiled then, not a big smile, but one that had Anna's heart thumping. It warmed his gray eyes, and gave his rugged face a boyish look. "I'm glad," he said. He held out his hand. "I'm Ben Thompson." The woman reached out her hand, and Ben grasped it firmly. It was soft and looked very small resting in his, he noted.

"I'm Arianna Jenkins," she replied. "Most people call me Anna."

Ben looked down and found himself gazing into eyes that were such a deep brown they reminded him of his favorite chocolate candy bar. They were so captivating it was difficult to look away. Anna herself solved that problem by lowering her lashes. Ben sensed her embarrassment, and with a slight squeeze he let her hand go. It fell slowly to her side. Ben tried to relieve the strange tension building between them. "I hope you weren't in a hurry to get anywhere," he commented.

Anna looked up again. "No," she said. "I was just on my way back to my hotel."

"Then you must be a visitor here?" Ben queried, already

knowing she was. He was acquainted with most of the area's population, it being such a small town.

"Yes. My mother lived here at one time. She asked me to come visit."

Ben's brow furrowed in thought. He didn't remember anyone having a daughter as lovely as this woman. Then again, if her mother didn't live here any more, it was more than possible that he wouldn't know who she was. But being a small town, people always knew when someone was visiting. He would have to consult his secretary on this one.

"Well, don't let me keep you," Ben said. Although reluctant to say good-bye, he had something to take care of himself. He gave her a hearty wave then continued up the hill.

Anna watched him go, absently rubbing her arms where he had held her. She felt rooted to the spot. What was it about that man? She had never been affected by a touch like that before. Not even when Lance first kissed her had she felt the electricity she felt when this man with the sober gray eyes touched her. Ben Thompson. The name wasn't familiar. But that wasn't surprising considering she really was not acquainted with many people.

She mentally forced herself to turn and walk back down the hill. She strolled leisurely through town without really seeing anything, her mind still on her encounter with Ben Thompson. He was very handsome in a rugged way, she mused. Apparently he spent a great deal of time outside, if his tan was any indication, and the muscles in his arms bespoke of hard work. He could be a local farmer, but from what she had heard concerning the lack of young farmers in the area she didn't think so. Despite his strength, he had seemed kind and gentle, so different from the men she knew.

Anna shook her head to rid herself of thoughts of Ben Thompson. The last thing she wanted was another man to complicate her life. She needed to concentrate on what she was going to do with her future. She dropped down onto a park bench in the town square with a silent groan. Until she made that promise to her mother, Anna's life had been perfectly mapped out. She would live in L.A., work for awhile, then someday marry the perfect man. But her time in Jordon made Anna see that there was a flaw in her plan.

She had wanted to be a photographer since her early teens, and had spent the ensuing years developing her talent. She was good and she knew it. Others knew it as well, and diligently pursued her with lucrative job offers. But she always resisted, and worked for herself, doing only those jobs she felt would help her achieve her goal of independence.

Recently she had begun to question her motivation. If not for her mother's illness and death she probably would have gone on skipping from assignment to assignment, pushing the nagging disquiet to the back of her mind. Since coming to Jordon the empty feeling she had been running from had returned full force. Anna knew she would have to find answers to her questions before she could go on.

The foremost question was what to do about her relationship with Lance, and the obvious answer was to end it. Would he accept that? she wondered. Probably not, she grinned ruefully.He was undoubtedly the most selfish person she had ever met, Anna finally admitted, although she had done her best to overlook it in the past. Well, Lance will just have to accept the fact that I'm not going to be part of his life anymore, Anna thought determinedly.

Sounds of the town slowly infiltrated Anna's consciousness. Eyes focused, she looked around, a smile lighting her face. She liked it here. She felt at home. The wind gently ruffled her long hair, the breeze cooling her heated skin. She drank in the noises of the small town. Children laughing, dogs barking, mothers calling their wayward offspring. People greeting one another; friendly. Anna suddenly realized how much she missed open, friendly people. People with nothing to hide, no secrets. I've spent too much time in the wrong company, she thought sadly.

She pushed herself off the bench and headed toward the hotel where she was staying. Although it wasn't a hotel in the true context of the word, it was quite nice. It had once been a private home, but had been converted to a beautiful, small hotel. Janice McCray, the owner, had done most of the decorating herself, so the hotel retained its comfortable, homey atmosphere.

Anna loved her room, one with a balcony that overlooked the extensive garden in the back. After dropping her backpack on the bed, she pulled open the french doors and stepped out onto the balcony, a place where she could think in private, and mentally search for the answers for which she was looking.

✠✠✠✠✠✠✠

Standing on the edge of the ridge, Ben Thompson looked down, his eyes focused not on the river flowing quickly below, but on the events of almost twenty years ago. He could still see Pastor Williams smile as the man looked into young Benny's eyes, could still hear him asking Ben to take his place. In the years since then, Ben thought he had finally ascertained what Pastor Williams meant. He was to take Pastor Williams' place among the people of this town, to lead the lost to Christ, the way Pastor Williams had led Ben. Ben had struggled against the call, but it was impossible to outwit God, and he had finally stopped fighting it.

The call into ministry had been soft at first, just a whisper in his heart, one he chose to ignore. He loved God, yes, but he was not willing to give his life to serve Him. That was during his teenage years. He wanted to be like the other boys, wild and carefree. Although he had tried, he never had truly been wild or carefree, not since Pastor Williams had given his life to save Ben's. The voice became louder and more persistent in college, so much so that Ben found himself driven to the mountains to get rid of it. It didn't work. After several months of denying God's call in his life, Ben finally acknowledged that he was meant to be a 'man of God'.

Never in a million years would he have guessed that his first church would be back in his hometown of Jordon, Virginia. It had taken him many years to forgive the people who had blamed him for the pastor's death, and driven him from his home.

But here he was, almost twenty years later, pastor of Jordon Baptist Church, in Jordon, Virginia. He worried he might have trouble with those who had accused him years before, but much to his surprise, the congregation welcomed him with open arms. It seems that God was working in other lives than just mine, Ben thought with a soft smile.

The first service he had conducted at the church brought healing for everyone. The people had been convicted of their wrong doings by Pastor Williams' replacement. He opened their eyes, enabling them to see how God had used the pastor to save a life just as Jesus sacrificed himself to save them.

Unfortunately, Ben hadn't heard about the change of heart. His mother had passed away from a heart attack a year after Ben had moved to Montana to live with his grandparents. So any connection he had with the town was totally severed until Ben was approached by Richard Weston to take the pastor position at his old church.

The search had been quick on the part of the church board. Ben's name had been brought to the attention of the church elders by the retiring pastor. Pastor Adkins had met Ben the previous year at a Bible conference. Ben had been excited to hear that his home church was doing so well, and spoke with Pastor Adkins at great length. Ben had no idea the man would bring his name before the congregation as his replacement. Ben's remembered promise to Pastor Williams prompted him to accept the position, and although it put his own dream on hold, he felt God's hand pushing him to return to his hometown.

The wounds had healed, as Pastor Williams had known they would, Ben thought with a wry grin. What a wise man. *I pray, Lord, that I may be as wise as he was.* Ben had been at the church for six months now, and was truly seeing a change both in his life and the lives of his congregation. He was a much fuller man, he felt, at least as far as his spiritual life was concerned. His prayers were vibrant and heartfelt, his walk with God was strong. But with all his success, there was a void in his life, a void he couldn't quite identify.

He had everything he thought he was supposed to have. He was positive he was where he was meant to be. The people of Jordan had forgiven him for his actions when he was a boy and accepted him as their shepherd. He had purchased a home on the outskirts of town with some acreage, and although it still needed some work, it was quite comfortable. So what was his problem?

Ben peered over the edge, down into the gorge where so many years ago a man had given his life for Ben. That thought still held him in awe, and never failed to evoke a vivid picture of Jesus dying for the sins of the world. Ben had experienced the truth, and now spent his life passing on the good news. But drat it all, he thought, slapping a hand on his thigh in frustration, what's missing?

He turned to make his way down the hill to where his pickup was parked. As he passed the place where he had run into Arianna Jenkins, he smiled. What a nice feeling to hold her, even if it had only been for a brief moment. Too bad I have no time to pursue the interest, he thought, getting into the pick-up and driving towards home. Never once did it occur to him to consult the God whose authority he was under.

Two

The insistent ringing of the telephone woke Anna out of a sound sleep. She groped for the receiver, finally managing to grasp it. Yawning, she mumbled a lazy "Hello."

Lance's angry voice brought her fully awake. "Where the devil are you and why weren't you here when I got back?" he demanded harshly.

If Anna hadn't been so shocked by his tone of voice, she may have wondered what business it was of his, but surprise robbed her of any quick come-backs. "My mother passed away several weeks ago, Lance, and she asked me to visit her hometown. So that's where I am. Jordon, Virginia. I did leave a message with your agent," she reminded him.

"I expected you to be here when I returned from the shoot. We have a few things to talk about, in case you've forgotten."

Anna bit her lip in dismay. She actually had forgotten. It seemed so long ago, that last fight they had had. The one just before Lance left to shoot his upcoming movie. His mentioning 'a few things' brought back all the nasty details in vivid color.

The evening had started like most of their other evenings together. Dinner at an exclusive restaurant. It always bothered Anna that Lance would only go to 'exclusive' places. She, herself, longed for a nice, romantic dinner for two, where they could be alone, not constantly interrupted by a stream of Lance's shallow friends. After the third such intrusion in less than ten minutes, Anna could hold her tongue no longer.

"Lance," she said, striving to keep her voice level, "do you think it would be possible for us to go somewhere else? I'm getting a little tired of your friends constantly dropping by our table." She hadn't thought it was such an outlandish request, but by the look on Lance's face, it was obvious he thought differently.

He gave her a haughty look, like a king might give to a common peasent. "This is the place to been seen, Arianna. I want to be seen. Why would I go anywhere else?"

That episode should have given Anna a clue as to what the rest of the evening would entail, but like so many times before, she swallowed her protests and went along with his game plan. What a fool, she thought later. She should have known what would happen. After dinner, they had gone to a party at one of Lance's friend's house where, of course, they were 'seen' again. He had asked her to take a few pictures of him with his 'friends' as publicity. She acquiesced to avoid a scene, actually thankful she would have something to do rather than play the humble girlfriend.

She took several roles of film, excitement building in her as it always did when she was behind her camera. She caught Lance in several activities, swimming, speaking with a group of men, feeding grapes to a young, and very beautiful, actress. She grimaced as she watched him cosy up to the voluptuous blonde, and finally had enough. She excused herself to Lance and escaped to the nearest restroom for a few moments of privacy. As she neared the door she unfortunately caught the tail-end of a conversation not meant for her to hear.

"Yeah," a male voice was saying. "Lance said he'd have her in bed by the end of the night for sure. He leaves for a shoot tomorrow and he wants some action before he goes."

A female voice countered. "The ice maiden hardly holds his hand in public. It's not likely she's going to give him a romp between the sheets."

"I don't know," the first voice declared. "Lance can be pretty persuasive. He said he'd let me know how it was. Maybe when she finds out what a let down he is in bed she might give me a try."

Anna melted into the darkness of the corridor before she was seen. Her face whitened at the thought that Lance would share such details with anyone, friend or no friend. She assumed he had accepted her refusal to sleep with any man other than her husband. Could it be possible that he was just biding his time, thinking she would eventually give in if he pressed the issue?

She stumbled out of the house towards the pool where Lance was talking to yet another up and coming star. "May I please speak to you," she whispered frantically. In irritation he tried to push her away, but she was adamant. Finally, he gave in, and after excusing them, he dragged her behind a cluster of bushes.

"What do you want?" His manner was less than understanding, but for once Anna was not in the mood to soothe his ruffled feelings.

"Just a few answers, Lance. Like the answer to the question of whether you're going to bed me tonight."

Lance gave a sly smile. "I knew you'd see it my way eventually," he whispered seductively. He reached for her, but she evaded his grasp.

"I'm also wondering who those nice people were outside the bathroom who seemed to feel it was their business to know what sex with me would be like."

Lance blanched at her comment. He obviously hadn't expected her to be so blunt. But Lance was still Lance, always looking out for himself. "Oh, I expect it will be very good," he smirked.

Anna's face burned with humiliation and anger. In fact, her anger was so fierce she had to stuff her hands in the pockets of her skirt to keep from slapping him. "You will never know Lance." She turned to walk away, but Lance grabbed her arm and pulled her to him.

"Don't count on that, babe," he ground out as his lips came down ruthlessly on hers. There was no tenderness in his kiss, only a fierce desire to possess. His arms crushed her in a cruel embrace. Anna was so stunned by the savagery of it all, she didn't try to fight until she felt one of his hands sliding to the front of her body. That sent her into action. Her fingers raked across his face, and when he let her go to cover his bleeding cheek, she punched him in the stomach with all her might, knocking the wind out of him, and sending him to the ground. As he lay sprawled at her feet, Anna made her escape.

Lance had called the next day to tell her how sorry he was. The drinks had gone to his head, he said, and would Anna please forgive him. Anna, having a soft heart and generally a non-confrontational attitude, told him she did. Lance seemed to think everything was fine, so when Anna told him that she would prefer not to see him again, he only laughed and said they would talk when he returned. He left for the movie set and Anna was called home by her mother. She had not seen Lance since then, and knew in her heart the relationship was well and truly over.

Lance's irate voice brought her back to the present. "You had better get your butt back here. I'm due back on location in two days. I want you here before I leave."

The aggression in Lance's tone made Anna recoil in fear and anger. His behavior had never been so commandeering before. But she was not some Hollywood groupie hanging on the man's every word. She had never been spoken to in that manner before. She certainly wasn't going to let it start now.

"I wasn't aware I was your slave girl to command, Lance," Anna said, her voice dripping in sarcasm. A choking sound came over the line, but Anna never even hesitated. "I am here. I intend to stay here. And you are more than welcome to go out to your shoot and stay there since I have no intention of ever seeing you again." She slammed the receiver down. "I hope that hurt you as much as it hurt me!" Anna mumbled, rubbing her tingling hand. She should know better than to let her temper get the better of her. She usually ended up in pain somehow.

A knock on the door got her attention. "Anna? Are you O.K. in there?" Janice McCray's voice floated through the closed door. The owner of McCray House was an older woman, a widow, who had decided to keep the hotel she and her late husband had renovated. Anna was thankful to have found such a nice place to live during her stay in Jordon.

"I'm fine, Mrs. McCray," Anna answered as she pulled on her robe and opened the door. "Just an annoying call."

The older woman entered the room and took a seat in the wing chair in front of the fireplace. This was Janice's favorite room, and she had gone all out when she redecorated it. It was done in green and white, with an ivy motif. Janice had done her best to make the room reflect the soothing garden she was so fond of. When Anna had come looking for a room three weeks ago, Janice had sensed the younger woman's need for peace and had purposely given her the 'garden room'. Now the peace that had settled around Anna during the last few weeks was totally disrupted.

"I wasn't aware anyone had your number here, dear," Mrs. McCray commented.

"I left the number with the man I had been dating, but I didn't really expect him to use it. I thought I had made myself plain, but he seems to have other ideas." Anna's frustration was evident as she paced the room. She worked her way from the balcony door to the bathroom door, then back again several times.

Mrs. McCray paused before speaking. She could tell Anna was truly agitated, but wasn't sure what to do about it. The young woman had become very important to Janice over the last three weeks, and she sensed her disquiet. "Perhaps he won't call back," she offered uncertainly.

Anna turned to look at the woman. She knew Mrs. McCray was trying to make her feel better, and felt a surge of gratitude. This woman was special to Anna, even after only three weeks of acquaintance. She reminded Anna of her own mother--warm, friendly, and caring. Mrs. McCray always left a light on in the lobby window when Anna was out late roaming the countryside. Anna's own mother had done that when Anna was out on an assignment. Anna could always count on Mama leaving a light burning for her, even when she returned in the middle of the night.

"Don't count on that, Mrs. McCray. Lance is an extremely determined man, and an incredibly selfish one. For some reason he seems to think having me around will further his career, which is all he really cares about." Anna looked out the window. "At least he's leaving for location again shortly. Maybe I can just ignore the phone for the next few days." She knew she would have to face Lance sooner or later, but later was much more preferable.

"Well," Mrs. McCray said, as she pushed herself out of her chair. "I came up here with some good news, actually. I found the house where your mother used to live. It was in the bank's possession for several years. They rented it out for awhile, but it's recently been purchased." Janice handed Anna a slip of paper with an address written on it. "It's on the outskirts of town, but fairly easy to get to. My friend didn't tell me who owns it now, but people around here are pretty friendly so you shouldn't have a problem if you want to take a look around."

Anna brightened considerably at the news. This was wonderful. She would finally see the place where her mother had spent her childhood. After Mrs. McCray left the room, Anna hurriedly showered before dressing in a pair of faded jeans and a cream cotton sweater. She pulled on her hiking boots and headed out to her Jeep Wrangler.

The ride out of town was pleasant and soothing to Anna's jangled nerves. The leaves were just beginning to bud on the trees, telling the world that spring had finally arrived. Anna's fingers itched to get to her camera and capture the beauty of the scenery around her. This would make a great coffee table book, she thought to herself. I could show Jordon in all four seasons. But then I would have to either keep coming back or stay for at least a year, her thoughts continued. Did she want to do that? What about her life in southern California? Before she had come up with any answers, she spied the address she was looking for on a mail box.

She pulled the Jeep over to the side of the road, just past the driveway, and took a good look around. So this is where her mother had grown up. Jackie Jenkins had said very little about her life here other than to tell Arianna that she had been happy. Anna was only just beginning to realize what her mother had given up for her husband.

The yard in front of the house was large, the house sitting a good distance from the road. There were flowers and shrubs on either side of the long drive, and also around the large front porch. The house itself was two stories, an old fashioned farm house. Definitely old. Janice had told her that the original house had been built over a hundred years ago. Even at such a great age, it was in marvelous condition. It was painted a sparkling white, with hunter green trim. There were flower boxes beneath all the front windows on both stories, overflowing with beautiful annuals.

Anna stared at the house, trying to picture her mother running around the yard as a child. She imagined a little girl who looked a great deal as Anna herself had when she was young, shimmying up the old maple tree at the side of the house. Perhaps Jackie had even used the tree to climb out her bedroom window, sneaking out to join her friends.

Wrapped up in her day dreams Anna didn't notice the man approaching her. He was practically leaning through her window before she even realized he was there. When Anna did turn she was so startled she jumped in her seat. Her hand went to her chest to quell her heart's frantic beating.

"I didn't mean to scare you," the man apologized, a smile lighting his gray eyes. He looked at her intently, wondering why she seemed so familiar. She was extremely attractive, there was no doubt about that. Her copper colored hair shone in the sun-light pouring through the top of the Jeep, its reddish tints glistening. Her eyes were a deep brown, like chocolate. Almost good enough to eat, Ben thought humorously. Then it hit him. Those were the same eyes he had gazed into the other day on the hill. This was the woman who had practically mowed him down.

Just as Ben had done, Anna was trying to place this man who had practically scared her to death. But unlike Ben, it only took Anna an instant to realize this was the man she had run into on the hill on the other side of town. And with the realization came a flood of red to her cheeks.

Ben noticed the color change immediately and was secretly amused. He hadn't seen a woman blush for a long time. But he didn't want to send this beautiful woman running before he found out why she was staring so intently at his house, so he tamped down his desire to laugh. "I hope you're not going to have a heart attack or anything," he said, trying to dispel the fright he could see lingering in her eyes.

It took a moment, but Anna recovered. "No, nothing like that." She drew in a deep breath. She hated being caught unaware. She wanted to explain herself before he could make any snap judgments about her. "I was just looking at your house."

Ben regarded her quizzically. Sure, it was a nice house, but not a show piece. "Any particular reason why?" he wanted to know. It might not be much, but it was the only place that was truly his, his sanctuary so to speak, and he wasn't about to let this strange woman, no matter how pretty she was, just roam around, especially if she was from one of the developers who were constantly nagging him to sell.

Anna mentally groped for a plausible explanation. She didn't want to appear foolish to this man, but there really was no getting around the point that she was trespassing on private land to fulfill a silly notion about seeing her mother's old home. Despite her misgivings, Anna decided that complete honesty would be the best way to approach the situation. "My mother lived here as a child, I was told, and I thought I would come out and see the place where she grew up." She took a breath. "I didn't mean to disturb you. I'll just be on my way."

She reached down towards the ignition, but her hand was captured by Ben's larger one. She looked into his eyes, and to her surprise his were smiling. "Wouldn't you like to take a look around, Miss Jenkins?" he offered.

Anna stared at him for a long moment. The hand holding hers was large and strong, but very gentle. Before she could answer, Ben took the car keys from her nerveless fingers and opened the door of the Jeep. "Since you put it so nicely, thank you." Anna smiled shyly when she recovered from her speechlessness. Ben handed back her keys, and helped her out of the car.

"I've only lived here for six months, so I really don't know the history. When I bought it, it had been empty for quite some time," Ben told her as they walked up the driveway. He led her to the porch steps. Anna stood on them, turning to look around. The photographer in her drank in the beauty of her surroundings. The daughter in her was saddened by the thought that her mother had never been able to return here.

"Come inside," Ben invited, gently cupping her elbow in his large hand. He guided her through the solid oak front door and into what was obviously the living room. It was large and cool, definitely a throw back to a time gone by. The room was paneled in cedar with a hardwood floor. The furniture was old, but in good condition. "I like old, comfy things," Ben explained, watching Anna as she scanned the room.

"It's very nice," Anna said truthfully, silently acknowledging their common like of 'old, comfy things'. She surveyed the room, trying to see it as it might have been so many years ago. The fireplace was made of fieldstone, most likely part of the original building. The mantle above it sported a few photographs, probably Ben's family.

"The kitchen, I think was added on later, as well as the upstairs. Whoever did it did a very good job." They walked into the kitchen which was indeed much more modern looking than the front room, although it was still very out dated. He noticed her hesitant look and laughed. "I decided to wait before doing any remodeling in here. I'm actually quite proficient on that old thing," he said, pointing to a stove that was probably older than Anna.

"I think I'd burn the house down if I tried to use it," she joked. "I'm much better with a microwave. Or better yet, having it delivered." Ben laughed again, sending little shivers down Anna's spine. She did her best to ignore it, but couldn't remember the last time she had been affected that way by someone's laugh.

Ben showed her the rest of the house. Upstairs there were three large bedrooms, and a fourth smaller room that Ben told her he had converted to a bathroom. "It's too far to go downstairs, especially in the middle of the night," he explained. All the rooms were tastefully furnished with older pieces that Ben told her had been left there when he moved in. "I wonder if some of these belonged to your mother?" Ben mused out loud.

Anna wondered that herself but didn't say anything. They finished their tour of the house then went outside by way of the back door. "The yard looks wonderful," Anna complemented him as they walked towards the big barn at the back of the yard.

"Thanks," Ben smiled at her. The barn was the original building, Ben explained, with some improvements. There were two horses inside, contently eating hay out of the manger. "The barn was in good shape, so there wasn't much that had to be done in here. The previous owners took very good care of the property. I don't recall the name since I bought it from the bank. It seems the family all died away without leaving any descendants, so the bank took over the house."

Anna roamed around the large interior, softly running her hands over boards that her mother had perhaps touched. She reached the ladder that led to the loft, and quietly asked permission to go up.

"Go ahead, but be careful, O.K.? That's one place I haven't been in yet and I'm not sure how safe it is."

She climbed up, letting her imagination run riot. Anna pictured her mother climbing up here when she was young, going to play in the hay loft. A smile lit her face when she reached the top. There wasn't much hay, but it was truly a child's paradise up here. There were a few old toys scattered around, and a rope tied to one of the rafters. She walked over to the door at the far end and opened it. She could see for miles. This must be where they dropped the hay out, Anna thought. I wonder if mom ever jumped out of here.

Anna reached for the rope and found that it was just the right length to swing out the door. The kids around here must have had a ball jumping in the hay from up here, Anna smiled to herself. She was oh, so tempted to do it herself, but the lack of hay at the end of the drop deterred her. Anna heard steps behind her, and turned to see Ben walking towards her.

"Some place, huh?" Ben asked as he joined her by the rope. "I sure hope you're not planning on jumping. I don't think I'm insured for ladies who jump out of hay lofts."

Anna couldn't help but laugh. "I have been considered a bit of a daredevil," she admitted. "But not even I'm foolish enough to jump out without the hay at the bottom."

"Good thing," Ben responded. He glanced at his watch. "I hate to end our tour, but I have an appointment in twenty minutes that I really can't miss, so I'm going to have to leave. You're welcome to look around the rest of the property if you'd like. In fact," Ben continued, "I should be back by one-thirty. Why don't you wander around for a bit, then have lunch with me?" What prompted him to ask her that he had no idea, but the more he thought about it the better it sounded.

Anna was hesitant. She really didn't know this man, and given her lack of discernment where men were concerned, she wasn't sure if it was such a good idea. But he seemed so nice. So was Lance when you first met him, Anna reminded herself sternly. Despite her mind's objections, her heart was telling her yes, and it was from her heart that she answered. "All right. That sounds great."

Ben let out the breath he didn't even realize he was holding. "Terrific. I'll give a holler when I get back, then I'll show you just how well I manage on the old cook stove." Before she could change her mind, Ben hurried off, scrambling down the ladder and rushing out of the barn. A few moments later Anna watched him pull around her Jeep on his way towards town.

Three

After Ben left, Anna slowly made her way out of the barn. She stood, leaning against the old, faded red structure, staring off in the distance. What to do next? Anna wondered. She really didn't know much about her mother's life, other than the fact that Jackie had said she had been very happy here. With no particular destination in mind, Anna pushed off the wall, wandered around the back of the barn, then headed toward the woods located beyond the small corral. Janice McCray had said the property was originally quite large, although she wasn't sure if it was still intact.

The woods were quiet except for the occasional bird singing. Anna enjoyed the peace, giving her a chance to collect her scattered thoughts. She would finish looking around then leave a polite note for Ben Thompson, telling him she had to get back to her hotel. It was a cop out, and Anna knew it, but for some curious reason Ben made her uneasy. It was nothing she could put her finger on. It was more on an emotional level. When he looked at her with those stunning gray eyes, it was almost as if he could read her mind. She was certain he knew she was hesitant about having lunch with him, so he had left quickly before she could change her mind.

Well, she would show him. A few more minutes then she would drive back to town. Anna strolled leisurely down the path, finally coming to a small creek gurgling through the woods. She stopped and looked around, the photographer in her taking over. The area was beautiful. Tree branches hung low over the quick running stream. Fish jumped, birds chirped, insects buzzed. Anna was enchanted. Had her mother enjoyed this same scene while she was a child? she wondered.

This would make a perfect picture, she thought. At times like these Anna wished her artistic talent was painting and not photography. Her fingers literally itched to put brush to canvas. She laughed quietly. She had tried painting once, and the results had been quite humorous. The instructor had barely been able to contain his laughter at Anna's attempt to capture a bird on canvas. Even Anna had to admit it was pretty funny. The bird looked more like a rat with wings, so she decided she had best stick to photography.

Anna sat down on the edge of the water, taking off her hiking boots and socks. She let her feet trail in the water and watched with fascination as small fish gathered around her toes, trying to nibble the unexpected intruders. She lay back on the bank, feet still resting in the water, and stared into the branches waving above her. It was so peaceful here, quiet and calm, so unlike her home in southern California. There was constant noise there, even at night. There were times it bothered Anna so much she pounced on any assignment that would get her out of town.

Her last assignment before her mother became ill had been in the mountains of northern California. She had spent several weeks scaling up cliffs, and down ravines, shooting a brochure for a travel club. It had been a wonderful experience, and blissfully quiet. It had been difficult for Anna to leave that place, and she had vowed to return. But it would have to wait.

Anna flipped over onto her stomach, resting her head on her arms. This area reminded her of her stay in the mountains, soothing her. Her eyes slowly closed, and soon she dropped off to sleep.

✠✠✠✠✠✠

Ben pulled into his driveway, relieved to see Anna's Jeep still out front. He hadn't been sure she would still be here despite the fact he had practically forced her to have lunch with him. She didn't appear to be a woman who would give in easily, and he assumed she would make a beeline for her hotel once he left. He had taken the precaution of speaking to Janice McCray while he was in town, and learned a little about his reluctant guest.

Arianna Jenkins was the daughter of Jackie Miller, who

was the only child of Horace and Mary Miller, the previous owners of this land. Janice didn't know much about Jackie's life once she had left Jordon, but had told him the woman had left with a man from California. Anna looked a great deal like her mother, if Janice's information was to be believed, so Jackie Jenkins must have been a beautiful woman, because Anna certainly was. That coppery hair and dark eyes were enough to turn the head of any man breathing.

Ben reined in his erratic thoughts. I don't have time to pursue a relationship, even if the woman in question is as beautiful as a sunrise, he reminded himself. His work with the church, not to mention the work he was doing on his home, kept him occupied almost every hour of the day. Most nights he fell into bed totally exhausted, which was exactly the way he wanted it. But he couldn't help wishing he could make time to see Anna on more than just a casual basis.

He jumped out of his truck, and walked purposefully towards the barn. It was very quiet, with no sign of Anna anywhere. He walked around the barn, following the tracks of her hiking boots into the wood. They led towards the creek, and soon he came upon Anna sleeping on the soft grass on the stream bank. He smiled softly. She was one gorgeous woman. He hated to disturb her, but by the look of her feet, she had been there awhile.

He bent down on his haunches, gently touching her hair, running his fingers lightly through it. Anna stirred, shivering slightly. My feet are freezing, she thought hazily, before rolling over and opening her eyes. She gazed up into Ben Thompson's face. For a minute she wasn't sure if he were real or just a continuation of the dream she had been having. Anna reached out a hand and came into contact with a very real person.

Ben smiled. "Hi, sleepy head." He held out his hand, helping her into a sitting position. "I would have let you sleep for a bit longer but your feet were turning blue." He reached out and took a foot into one of his large hands. He frowned, then began rubbing her foot between his hands.

"You don't have to do that," Anna said breathlessly. His touch was warming more than just her foot. She could feel the heat all the way up her body.

Ben was still frowning. "You're lucky your feet aren't frozen by now. How long have you been here?"

Anna glanced down at her watch, then gave a startled yelp. "I can't believe it! It's been over an hour."

The frown turned to a scowl. He abruptly thrust her boots and socks into her lap and scooped her up in his arms. "That was a very foolish thing to do," he admonished.

Anna glared up at him. "I wasn't cold until you woke me up."

"Lady, you'd have been blue from head to toe if I hadn't woken you up." He strode quickly down the path, Anna in his arms. He didn't speak again, and Anna was hesitant to say anything. Ben was not looking very pleased, and Anna, already feeling every bit as foolish as Ben thought she was, didn't want to cause any more problems.

Ben had calmed down by the time they reached the house. He looked down at the woman held in his arms, and caught her watching him cautiously. A lop-sided grin appeared on his face. "Sorry about that," he apologized, as he deposited her on a kitchen chair. "Guess I shouldn't have gotten quite so bent out of shape." He looked deep into her eyes. "But it was a very dangerous thing to do, Anna."

"I know," Anna replied in a small voice. "I can't believe I fell asleep."

Ben placed her feet in a pan of warm water and began gently rubbing them. "I can. It's a very tranquil place. I've done it myself. Except I don't stick my feet in ice cold water."

"You don't know what you're missing," Anna quipped, relieved that the tension was gone.

Ben looked at her and laughed. "Since I now have you pretty much a prisoner," Ben said, "I guess I'll get lunch started." Anna began to protest, but Ben held up his hand. "You shouldn't go anywhere until your feet warm up, and that could take awhile.

Besides, I'm holding your shoes hostage until you agree."

"Well," Anna dragged out, "I guess if you put it that way, I'll stay."

Despite the strained beginning, Anna enjoyed her lunch with Ben very much. He was an amusing person, making Anna laugh with stories of his childhood. He gave Anna a brief history of himself, although he left out the part about Pastor Williams and the promise. He still had trouble talking about that time of his life, even though he was sure Anna would not condemn him as others had.

Anna, for her part, listened attentively, feeling a growing admiration for the man. He had chosen to follow God's call, and she was impressed with his dedication in pursing that call. "Is it difficult to work here, I mean since most of these people knew you when you were little."

Anna's question caught Ben off guard. No one had ever asked him that before, and he wasn't sure how to answer without telling her about the accident at the ridge. Just thinking about it caused his heart to ache. "Well," he hesitated. "I've never really considered it before," he answered. That much was true. When he decided to accept the position, he hadn't given it a thought. "I left when I was ten, and so much has changed since then."

Anna looked at him curiously. He wasn't telling her the whole story, she could tell. Her own turmoil made her sensitive to the emotions of others, and in Ben she sensed hidden pain. Despite knowing him a very short time, Anna had the strangest desire to ease the pain he was trying so hard to hide.

"So why are you in Jordon," Ben asked, deftly changing the subject.

"I made a promise to my mom," Anna told him, amazed she would share that with someone who was almost a total stranger. "That's really the only reason I came to Jordon," Anna reiterated, finishing her coffee. "I promised. I don't know why it was so important to her. She never even spoke about her life here except after she became ill."

"Perhaps she felt you needed to know."

Anna contemplated that for a moment before she spoke. "Maybe. Mom was very happy here, I could tell by the look on her face as she was telling me about it. She also told me why she left. In her own way I think she was trying to warn me about Lance."

Ben looked up from his empty plate at that comment. Just who was Lance? he wanted to know."Who might Lance be?" Ben questioned, hoping the query sounded casual.

"He's the man I was dating. Let's just say he reminded my mother a lot of my father."

"And that's not good, I take it."

"No." Anna did not elaborate on the comment, leaving Ben to wonder exactly what kind of man Lance was. Before he could question her further, she was up, bare feet padding over to the sink. "I really need to get back, Ben," she said. She turned to face him, once again smiling. "Do you think I could have my socks and shoes back now?"

Ben looked down at her bare toes and smiled. "I don't know. Your feet are so cute, why cover them up?"

Anna laughed. "Ben. Feet are not cute. They are feet, and they are cold feet to boot."

"Oh, all right, spoil sport. I'll give them back. But only on the condition that you have dinner with me tomorrow night." He held his breath waiting for her answer

"That's hardly fair," she told him. "I already had lunch with you because of the shoe hostage thing." He glanced sharply at her, then smiled at the teasing look on her face.

"But that was to pay me back for carrying you," he informed her.

"I never asked you to carry me," she said primly. "Is it my fault you decided to act like a he-man?"

Ben looked insulted. "I do not act like a he-man."

Anna grinned. "Well, maybe not. But I'm still not sure about dinner," her voice was serious now.

"Think of it like a business dinner. I can tell you about the area, and you can get a feel of what it was like twenty years ago."

He tried his best to convince her it was a good idea.

She pondered his suggestion. He had a point. She did want to learn about Jordon, and it had been a long time since she had spent time with anyone as interesting as Ben. Her time with Lance was usually spent trying to avoid his hands. She was sure it wouldn't be like that with Ben. "All right. That sounds like fun. But since you made lunch, I'll do dinner. I'll pick you up at six-thirty." Before she could change her mind, or Ben could argue about it, she hurried out the door.

Ben stood there, staring at the spot she had just vacated. What had he gotten into? He was actually going to let a woman take him out to dinner. It could be fun, he thought as he absently washed out his coffee cup. In fact, it might prove to be quite entertaining. "But I refuse to let her pay for dinner," he announced out loud.

Anna pulled her Jeep into its spot in the hotel parking lot and sat there staring into space. Her mind wandered over the last few hours and she smiled. Ben Thompson was a man to be reckoned with, Anna realized. How easily she had let him talk her into dinner tomorrow. She was usually a fairly good judge of character, Lance being an exception, and her instincts told her that, as a gentleman, Ben would never allow her to pay for dinner. Well, we'll just see about that, Anna thought to herself. I still have a few tricks up my sleeve.

"Anna," Janice called as Anna was passing the reception desk. "You had another call while you were out." She handed Anna a folded slip of paper. "The man seemed rather upset."

Anna read the note then crushed it in her hand. Why would that man not take no for an answer, she wondered. "Don't worry about it Mrs. McCray. Lance will just have to accept my decision to remain here for now."

Janice smiled. "So you're going to stay? That's wonderful."

"Well, I did promise my mom I would visit. It's proven to be much more enjoyable than I thought it would be. Jordon is so beautiful, it's given me a great idea for another book. That's where I'm headed actually," Anna told Janice. "I need to write a few things down. I can't believe I forgot my camera and notebook earlier."

The two women walked up the stairs together. "I'm glad you're going to stay. It will be nice to have company."

Anna turned to Janice and smiled. This woman had been so kind to her. "I don't believe for a minute that you are lonely. There is hardly a second that goes by that you're not involved in something or other."

"True, true," the older woman agreed. "But now I'll have something right here to keep me occupied."

"What do you mean 'keep you occupied'?" Anna questioned. She had a sinking feeling that Mrs. McCray might try to play matchmaker.

"Oh, nothing." She quickly changed the subject. "What are your plans for dinner today? I thought we could share some barbeque out in the garden."

"That sounds great, Mrs. McCray," Anna replied. She opened the door to her room. "Why don't I run out and get some of those yummy cookies at the bakery?"

"No need for that. I already made a batch. And please, Anna," Janice put her hand on Anna's arm. "Please call me Janice." The woman smiled gently.

Anna faced the woman, then gave her a big hug. "Thank you so much," her voice husky, "Janice."

She sat at her desk for the next hour, jotting ideas in her notebook. Although her feet had warmed up, Anna still felt chilled. She was embarrassed that someone as experienced as she was in the outdoors had allowed her feet to remain in freezing water while she fell asleep. Too much on my mind, she excused herself. She took a long soak in a hot tub, then dressed in a faded pair of sweats. Out the French doors she saw Janice in the garden, grilling chicken on a gas barbeque. Her Irish Setter, Hetty, ran in circles around her, every once in awhile chasing after a roaming squirrel.

Anna felt a grin tugging her lips. She couldn't remember

the last time her heart had felt so light, or a time when she laughed or smiled so much. She had become much too serious over the last few years. She chose not to reflect on those times right now, but soon she was going to have to examine her life, and decide if she was going in the right direction.

Anna hurriedly finished dressing, then rushed down the stairs. When she walked out into the garden, Hetty came bounding towards her. Anna was Hetty's favorite playmate, one who never failed to romp with the playful pup. Tonight was no exception. She gave Hetty a ruffle behind the ears, and Hetty, for her part gave Anna big sloppy kisses. Then Anna tossed a stick far out into the yard, and the games began. Over and over she threw, and over and over Hetty brought it back, only stopping when Janice called them both to dinner.

After she gave thanks for the food, Janice began questioning Anna about her afternoon. "Did you meet the owners," she asked nonchalantly, knowing very well she had.

Anna hesitated a moment. "I met the owner. His name is Ben Thompson. He's the pastor of your church, I believe," she answered, sliding a look over at Janice.

"Oh, really," Janice replied in seeming surprise.

Anna couldn't contain herself any longer and burst out laughing. Janice was trying so hard not to sound interested, when Anna knew very well the woman was practically dying for details. "Janice, you're a treasure. I met Ben when he practically gave me a heart attack by sneaking up on me. He showed me around the house and barn. He had to leave, but invited me to lunch, so I had lunch with him. That was all," she added before Janice could question her further. "But I am taking him to dinner tomorrow night," Anna couldn't help baiting her.

"You're taking him to dinner?"

"Don't sound so surprised. I owe him for lunch. Besides, he promised to tell me some more about the town, which will be helpful for both my pursuits. I consider it more a business dinner than anything else."

Janice grimaced. That was not what she wanted to hear,

but she didn't want to press Anna any farther. She would just have to bide her time. "Well, I'm sure it will be profitable for both of you," she proclaimed.

They passed the remaining time in idle conversation, then cleared off the picnic table. Janice invited Anna to join her in her sitting room, but Anna declined. She was rather tired, and felt an early night would do her good. She bade good-night to Janice then headed up to her room. In no time she was cuddled beneath the covers, and nodding off to sleep, visions of sparkling gray eyes filling her dreams.

Four

A sunbeam shining in her face woke Anna the next morning. She stretched luxuriously, then turned over to stare out the window. It was a beautiful day. For some reason Anna couldn't understand, she felt an excited rush surge through her. Then it came to her. She was suppose to take Ben Thompson out to dinner tonight.

Anna jumped out of bed. There was so much she wanted to accomplish today, the first being making dinner reservations. She had an inkling Ben was the kind of man who would insist on paying for the meal even though she had asked him and, although she normally wouldn't object, she wasn't comfortable letting him pay. He might think she was carrying a flag for woman's rights, but in truth Anna felt frightened about being in debt to Ben. He stirred feelings in her that no man had ever done before, and she barely knew him. She had to keep him at arm's length if only to keep her peace of mind.

She rushed through her shower, then hurried downstairs to consult with Janice. Anna wanted to take Ben somewhere nice, but not romantic. Not being familiar with the restaurants in the area, she approached Janice with her dilemma.

"There's a new place over on Main Street, right downtown. It used to be a flower shop, but it closed down some time ago. New owners came in and made it into a nice little coffee house. They have a limited menu, but the food is excellent, and they're moderately priced. I've been there a few times and have enjoyed it."

"Sounds perfect, Janice, thanks," Anna gave the woman a quick hug. She ran back upstairs to grab her camera bag. Janice volunteered to make the reservations, so Anna was free to get on with the rest of her day, which consisted mainly of getting some shots of Jordon in spring. She hopped into the Jeep, and set out.

Anna drove around town snapping pictures out the Jeep's window, just to get a feel of the town itself. The streets were crowded, it being Saturday. People greeted each other and kids ran around the town square waiting for their parents to finish whatever they were doing. Adults laughed and chatted. Anna caught it all on film. But with each picture she took, her heart became heavier, and she couldn't figure out why.

After an hour she could stand no more, and headed the Jeep to the outskirts of town. She found herself walking back up the hill, the one where she had first met Ben. As she climbed the gentle slope, tears began to fall down her cheeks. Soon her eyes were so misted with tears she couldn't see where she was going. She stumbled to a stop, and let the sobs come. There was no way to stop the torrent of emotions running through her.

She cried for her mother, and the life she had given up to marry a man who had no concept of commitment. But mostly she cried for herself. She felt so empty inside, desperate to know what was missing. She thought she had it all. Her career was well on its way giving her financial security She had many friends, and when she chose, she didn't lack male companionship. So what was missing? Why was she so miserable?

Anna sat for several minutes, her head resting on her knees, waiting for the tears to abate. She felt a faint stirring in her heart, but couldn't put her finger on exactly what it was. Although she tried for some time, the cause remained elusive. Anna finally gave up. She trudged back down the hill, then retreated to the sanctuary of her hotel room.

Janice was out when Anna returned, but the girl at the desk assured Anna that reservations had been made for her and Ben at the "Flower Shop" for seven o'clock. "There's also a letter for you," the girl said, handing an envelope to Anna.

Anna took the envelope, curious as to who would be sending her a letter. Glancing at the return address, she noticed it was from her friend and publisher, Lauren Hiller. Anna ripped it open, and a single sheet fell out. On it were instructions to meet her in Williamsburg on Monday, no greeting, no signature.

Hello to you to Lauren, Anna thought to herself and grinned. Lauren had such a one-tracked mind when it came to work. "Thanks," she told the girl, then hauled her heavy camera bag upstairs.

Anna's somber mood began to disperse soon after she entered her room. The lovely garden decor never failed to lift her spirits. She tossed the bag on the bed, and dug out the exposed film. Janice had kindly approved Anna's use of an extra bathroom as a darkroom, so Anna grabbed up the film and closeted herself in her make-shift darkroom.

The shots she had taken came out better than she had hoped. Excitement again built inside her as each image became exposed. Ideas began flowing through her brain, and she hastily wrote down a rough outline. She'd bet her next paid assignment that this book would be a hit, not only with the locals, but with anyone who had a yen for small town life.

Anna came out of the bathroom with a huge grin, her earlier misery almost forgotten. She glanced down at her watch and gasped. It was nearly six. She'd have to hurry if she planned to get to Ben's by six-thirty.

Pulling out her one nicely casual outfit, Anna hastily dressed, then did a quick make-up job. She pulled her hair into a knot at the top of her head, thrust her feet into a pair of flats, then ran out the door.

"Have a nice time, dear," Janice called, as Anna raced past the reception desk. She laughed as Anna flung her arm in greeting. Running a little late, Janice chuckled to herself.

Anna pulled into Ben's driveway just past six-thirty. Not too bad, she thought, as she climbed out of the vehicle and sauntered up to the front door.

Ben was thinking almost the same thing, although his thoughts were in reference to Anna. Her red silk polka dot skirt and cream sweater were a nice change to the jeans she had been wearing on her previous visit. Little wisps of coppery hair escaped the knot on her head and curled around her face. In all, the picture she presented was quite beautiful. Ben found his heart beating just a little bit faster than normal, which surprised him. He didn't exactly lack female company when he wanted it. In fact, to his embarrassment, his company was much coveted by the unmarried women at the church. But he had never encouraged any relationship, feeling it would interfere with his promise to Pastor Williams.

Now here he was, going to dinner with a most beautiful, and rather mysterious, woman. Who'd have figured? he thought, shaking his head. He opened the door to greet his guest. "A bit late, aren't we, Miss Jenkins?" he questioned, eyebrow raised.

"Well, Reverand Thompson, I've always believed in being fashionably late," Anna replied with a straight face. "Are you ready to go?"

Ben smiled."Ready and waiting," he said, hoping the truth of his statement would go unnoticed. He closed and locked the door and followed Anna back to the Jeep. He held her door before getting in himself. "Where are we going? Or am I not suppose to ask?"

Anna turned as she backed the Jeep out of the drive. "You can ask, but that doesn't mean I'll tell you." She drove back towards town.

"Can I guess?" Ben wondered.

"I don't know, can you?" she bantered.

"Let me see," Ben mused. "There aren't a great deal of choices, unless of course were going out of town." He looked to Anna for confirmation, but her face gave him no clues. "There is that new place, but I don't know if they serve dinner. I know," Ben snapped his fingers, "we're going to McDonalds."

Anna laughed. "I only go to McDonalds for the diet Coke. I rarely eat there." She pulled the Jeep into a parking spot in front of the Flower Shop. "We're here."

Ben looked confused. "A flower shop. I thought we were going to have dinner. Are you buying me flowers, too?"

"No, silly. This is it. Janice assures me the food is wonderful." Anna unbuckled and opened the door of the Jeep. Ben was there to give her a hand out. "Thank you."

"You're very welcome," Ben said softly, squeezing her hand. He pulled it through his arm and they walked together into the restaurant.

The interior of the building still retained the aura of a flower shop. There were plants everywhere, as well as bouquets of flowers. Ben and Anna were led to a table close to the front window, where they could look out onto the street. There was a large bouquet of fresh carnations in red, pink and white sitting on the table.

Ben pulled out her chair and Anna sat down. She leaned over, closing her eyes, and took a deep breath. The fragrance from the flowers filled her. Sitting back in her chair with a sigh of appreciation, she noticed Ben staring at her. Anna raised an eyebrow in question, but Ben only smiled.

The waiter appeared to take their order, then they were left alone. "What did you do with yourself all day?" Ben asked, taking a sip of his water. He was curious to know how she spent her time, since he knew she had only come to Jordon to fulfill her promise to her mother.

"Actually, I was working, which is why I was late," Anna answered him.

Ben looked at her in surprise. "What do you do that you can work here all day? I thought you were only visiting."

The waiter, depositing their soft drinks on the table, delayed Anna's reply. She took a long sip of her soda before speaking. "I'm a freelance photographer," she announced.

Her answer intrigued Ben Although he really hadn't given it much thought, that was not what he expected to hear. He envisioned photographers as big and brawny men skulking through darkest Africa, not petite, beautiful redheads roaming his hometown. "That's a rather unusual occupation," he commented. "How did you get into it?"

Anna smiled. "I've always enjoyed taking pictures. When I was in junior high my mom bought me a 'real' camera, you know, with the lens you have to focus yourself, and all that. She figured I'd give up when I found out how much work it really was."

"I take it you didn't. Give up, I mean."

The smile on Anna's face grew. "No, much to her astonishment. Normally, I would try something for a week or two, then give it up because it was too much like work. But not this. It gives me a wonderful feeling to be able to capture special moments of time. I started by taking pictures for the yearbook at school. I branched out to photograph parties for friends, and just continued on from there."

The arrival of their dinner interrupted the conversation. Ben gave a short blessing, before continuing. "What do you do now? High school year books? Portraits?"

Anna made a face. "Hardly. My last assignment was a brochure for backpackers. I went up into the mountains of northern California with a guide to photograph trails and such."

"Do you enjoy it? The photography, I mean."

She considered for a minute before answering. "Yes," Anna said slowly, "I enjoy it very much. When I'm out in the middle of nowhere, by myself for the most part, I'm able to see things in a whole new light. The places I go are soothing, peaceful."

"I know what you mean," Ben agreed. "When I lived in Montana my grandfather took me hiking several times every year. It brought me closer to him, but it also brought me face to face with God and His creation. It was on one of those trips that I felt God calling me to enter the ministry."

Anna was startled by Ben's reference to God. She had never really given it much thought before. She believed in God, of course, but didn't believe He was much interested in her or the decisions she made concerning her life. Ben went on to talk about some of his trips, but Anna only half paid attention to him. She was still musing over his previous remarks.

"Anna,"Ben said softly. He had noticed her quietness, and had kept up a meaningless flow of small talk to cover her inattention. But now that they were finished eating he felt it was time to help her out of her introspective mood. "Why don't we go back to my place for coffee," he suggested when he had her attention.

"Sure, that sounds great," Anna readily agreed. Ben was surprised that she gave in to his suggestion so easily considering how much he had to finagle just to get her to go to dinner. But he wasn't about to argue the point.

The waiter left the receipt on the table. Ben made to pick it up, but Anna forestalled him. "It's already been taken care of," she told him.

"Oh?" he questioned.

"I had a feeling you might object to a woman paying for your dinner, so I prepaid. The manager was surprised, but not objectionable to the idea." Anna grinned triumphantly at Ben, who made a face in reply.

When they reached the car, Ben led Anna to the passenger side. "I was wondering if you would let me drive. I've always wanted to drive a Jeep." Ben eyes glowed with excitement, making him look like a little boy at Christmas.

Anna laughed. "O.K. But don't get out of control. I happen to love this Jeep, and want it to remain in the sterling condition it's in." He didn't say respond other than to hold out his hand for the keys. Anna dropped them in his outstretched palm, then waited for him to get in.

Ben started the Jeep and drove away from the curb. It had been years since he had driven any type of off-road vehicle, but the sheer enjoyment of it came flooding back. "This is great," he called over the sound of the engine . "Mind if I take her through the field behind my house?" Ben asked. He looked over at Anna hopefully.

She could see how much he was enjoying himself and didn't have the heart to say no. "Just be careful."

"Yes, mother."

Anna couldn't remember the last time she had so much fun. Ben was a good driver, almost as good at controlling the Jeep as she was. He went up hills, through small streams,basically having a ball, but always considerate of the fact that Anna was not exactly dressed for baha driving. After half an hour he headed back towards the house. "I did promise coffee," he told her when she asked if he was finished already. "Plus the fact that I might get addicted, and I can't afford a Jeep yet."

The evenings were still chilly, so Ben lit a fire in the fireplace. They sat on the sofa , Anna at one end and Ben at the other. Anna slipped her shoes off and curled her feet up under her skirt, turning to face Ben. Picking up her mug, she took a long sip of the steaming brew. When she looked up, Ben was watching her intently.

"What?" she questioned. "Do I have a coffee mustache?"

Ben smiled softly, but didn't answer for a moment. When he did speak Anna almost wished he had kept quiet. "You were very thoughtful at dinner tonight. Was there anything wrong?"

He watched Anna carefully, knowing it was their conversation about God that had caused her introspection. From what his grandfather told him, Ben had that same confused look on his face when his grandfather had talked to him about Jesus. Ben didn't know what Arianna's spiritual life was like, but he was willing to bet that she had never accepted the Savior into her life.

Anna hesitated. She wasn't really certain how to respond. Although she was conscious that there was something wrong in her life, she didn't know how to express the problem. The empty feeling inside her had been there for so long it had become a part of her, and she wasn't sure how to go about changing it.

Ben waited patiently. He sensed her struggle, and began praying silently. *Lord Jesus, please help Arianna realize her need of you. Help her see what is missing in her life*. His prayers were interrupted when Anna spoke.

"I'm not sure how to reply, Ben." She tried to laugh, but failed. "There's just so much happening to me so fast." Unable to stop them, tears began to trickle down her cheeks.

Ben scooted over to take Anna in his arms. They tightened around her, and Anna's tears flowed faster, until she was sobbing. He pulled her into his lap, and just held her, trying to stem the trembling of her body. "Oh, Arianna," he sighed, feeling her pain.

"I'm sorry," she hiccuped, trying to control her sobs.

He ran his fingers gently through the hair that had escaped from the confines of the knot. "There's nothing to be sorry for, honey," he comforted. His arms tightened momentarily, before letting her go. He slid her gently off his lap, then stood. He took her hands and lifted her from the sofa, pulling her gently into his embrace.

"Let me tell you a story," Ben said quietly somewhere over the top of her head. "When I was ten, there was an accident on the ridge. I had dropped my ball over the edge and had gone down to get it, getting stuck in the process. Pastor Williams heard me crying and rescued me. But trying to push me up caused him lose his balance. He fell and was killed. He gave his life to save mine." He looked down into Anna's somber brown eyes. "I realized then what it meant to sacrifice yourself for another person. He showed me the love of Jesus."

Anna gazed up into Ben's face and saw the pain in his gray eyes. She knew that this was what was at the bottom of the pain she had seen in his eyes the first day she met him. Knowing how difficult it was for him, Anna wondered why he was telling her. She only had to wait a moment before Ben enlightened her.

"It was years before I really understood what it all meant. When I was a teenager I got into a lot of trouble. Nothing horribly serious, but still trouble. My grandfather took me hiking for the first time then. We went into the mountains, and there it all became clear. My problems stemmed from the emptiness I felt inside me. I thought at first it was just because my mom died. But that wasn't it. My grandparents were wonderful, giving and showing me all the love I needed.

"Then my grandfather told me about Jesus. He had never said much about it before then because he knew the time wasn't right. My heart was too hard. But out there in the beauty of God's creation, where there was nothing between me and Him, I realized what was missing. I was missing Jesus. When I accepted Him into my heart, the emptiness disappeared."

Anna's eyes grew large with wonder. Could it really be that simple? She had heard the message of Jesus before, that he was sent as a Savior for men. She had accepted Him as a child, but had long ago turned away from her childhood faith. Was that what was missing? Was the Lord telling her that she had strayed too far?

"But how do you know He's there?" Anna questioned, her voice low.

For an answer Ben led her out the front door and stood with her on the grass. Holding her with one arm, he used his other hand to gently tilt her face to the sky. "Look up, Arianna," he whispered. "Look up and tell me that He isn't here."

Anna stared at the stars twinkling in the clear night sky. There were millions of tiny pinpoints of light. The beauty of it touched her like it never had before.

"By the word of the Lord were the heavens made, and all the host of them by the breath of his mouth." Ben quoted the verse in Psalms with conviction, love of the Lord ringing in his voice. "He made all this with his hand, but as beautiful as it is, man is so much more to Him. He sent his Son, not for the stars, but to die for all mankind, Arianna. For you."

Suddenly Anna felt so weary, the weight of the world seemingly resting on her slim shoulders. She drooped in Ben's arms, until he was holding her up. "I'm sorry Ben," she whispered, her voice a bare thread. "This is just too much right now. I just can't take it in."

Ben bent and softly kissed the top of her head. "That's all right, Arianna," he told her. "Believe me, I understand. Just think about it, all right?"

"I'll try," she answered.

"That's all I ask."

He held her a few minutes more, then Anna pulled away. "I need to get back," she explained, when his look questioned her.

Ben nodded his head in agreement, but his heart wasn't in it. Anna had felt so good in his arms, he was unwilling to let her go, although he knew it was for the best. As a Christian, particularly a Christian pastor, he knew he couldn't get involved with a non-believer, and he wasn't sure where Anna stood spiritually.

He went into the house to retrieve her shoes and purse, then walked with her to the Jeep and helped her in. "Call me when you get in, O.K.?" he asked. "I want to know that you got back all right."

"You don't have to worry, Ben. I'll be fine."

"I'm sure you will be, but humor me anyway, all right?"

Anna gave a wobbly smile. "O.K." She backed out of the drive, and raising a hand, gave Ben a feeble wave good-bye. When she was out of sight of his house, she eased the Jeep to the side of the road, and dropped her head in her hands. A few hours with one man, and the shallow facade of her life was in tatters. He had opened the door to memories she had locked deep inside her, and there was no way to stuff them all back in. As much as Anna wanted to hide, she knew she had to face them to be able to move on with her life.

No matter how hard she tried, Anna could not hold back the tears. They flowed freely, and the pain of the last few years flowed with them. She faced the onslaught of memories, let them come to her. As she did so a calmness settled over her. She wasn't sure how it happened, but she found herself offering up a prayer for the first time since she was a young child.

"Lord, I know now what you've been trying to tell me for so long. Please forgive me for ignoring you, for shutting you away for all these years. Fill this empty spot inside me." Anna lifted her head and wiped the tears from her cheeks. Although she was still very weary, she felt the heavy burden being lifted off her shoulders. A peaceful smile lit her face. She restarted the Jeep and drove back to the hotel, smile firmly in place.

Janice had already gone to bed when Anna walked through the lobby and climbed the stairs to her own room. She stood on the balcony, gazing up at the starlit sky, letting the peace of the night wash over her. It was nearly midnight by the time she folded herself under the down comforter, immediately falling into a deep and peaceful sleep.

Minutes later her restful slumber was interrupted by the

ringing of her beside phone. “Hello,” she whispered.

“I seem to remember asking you to call,” a voice said softly, taking any sting out of the words.

Anna was instantly awake. “Oh, Ben, I am so sorry. I completely forgot!”

“No kidding,” he joked. “Are you all right?” Ben questioned on a more serious note.

She smiled in the dark. “I’m fine. I want to thank you for what you shared with me tonight.” Anna did not enlighten him farther. Her emotional state was still fragile, and she didn’t feel up to another emotional scene.

“My pleasure, sweetheart,” the endearment flowed easily off his lips. He drew in a deep breath. “As long as you’re O.K. I’ll let you go.”

“Thanks for calling Ben. I am sorry.”

After hanging up the phone, Anna laid back down and smiled up at the ceiling, her thoughts on Ben Thompson. He was so different from the other men she knew. He was willing to make himself vulnerable in order to help others. She had no idea what she was doing, getting involved with him, but she couldn’t seem to help the feelings beginning to surface concerning this man. She would just have to trust in her newfound faith in the Lord, that He knew where the relationship was headed.

Anna’s lips tilted up. It felt wonderful knowing there was Someone she could turn to no matter what. With that thought she drifted back to sleep.

Five

Anna awoke to another beautiful spring day. Rolling over, she glanced at the clock sitting on the bedside table, then jumped out of bed. It was only seven-thirty. If she hurried she might be able to go to church with Janice. Even though she was uncomfortable about sharing her experience last night with Ben, she had the greatest desire to praise the Lord in a church with other believers. The fact that it was Ben's church made her a little nervous. Anna didn't want him to think she was chasing him. Perhaps she could convince Janice to slip out as soon as the service was over.

She rushed through her shower, then slipped on the only other dress she had with her. It was a white ankle-length dress, that flowed around her legs when she walked. Wearing it always made her feel wonderful. She slipped it over her head and let the folds of white silk caress her body. Running a brush through her long hair, Anna pulled the sides up with a comb, letting the rest fall down her back. She thrust her feet into white heels, then headed downstairs, where she knew Janice would be having breakfast.

Janice raised an eyebrow when she saw Anna coming towards her. "You look very nice, dear," she commented. "Going anywhere special?"

"Actually," Anna said, pulling out a chair and sitting down, "I thought I would go with you to church this morning."

"I'd enjoy that. What made you decide to come?" Janice was never one to beat around the bush, a trait which Anna found refreshing after all the subterfuge of the Hollywood scene.

"I finally realized what was missing," came Anna's somewhat cryptic reply. Janice waited patiently, knowing there was more. "Last night, Ben told me a little about his childhood. He helped me see that Jesus was what was missing in my life."

Janice came around the table and gave Anna a big hug. "I was afraid you'd leave before you learned that lesson," she admitted, tears in her eyes.

There were tears in Anna's eyes as well. "I know. Thank you for being patient with me." She laughed shakily. "I hope I didn't try you too much."

"Of course not dear," Janice said, sitting back down. "I'm just so thankful you've come back to Him."

Anna was curious. "How did you know that I knew Him in the first place?"

"Your mother told me. I haven't been totally honest with you dear," Janice admitted. "I knew your mother slightly before she left town. I moved here just before she moved away. Although we never really kept in touch, your mother sent me a letter about six months ago. She knew she was going to die, and she wanted me to help you get back on the right track. Jackie was very worried about you."

Hanging her head, Anna said, "I know. I know I was a trial to her during the last few years. I just couldn't seem to stop the restlessness. Then when I started going out with Lance..." She left the sentence unfinished and groaned.

Janice laughed. "Don't worry, honey. We all make mistakes. Your mama knew that. That's why she was so concerned for you. She could see in you what she herself went through as a girl. But she also knew that you were a much stronger person than she was, and it wouldn't be long before your eyes were opened."

"I'm glad she had so much confidence in me."

The two women smiled at each other then quietly finished their breakfast, before leaving for church. Janice led them through the sanctuary, and took a seat near the front where Ben was sure to see them. Anna frowned slightly at Janice's obvious maneuvering. The woman was practically pushing Anna into Ben's arms. Poor Ben. Being single, especially a single pastor, could be a problem, particularly when he was so attractive.

Anna didn't have the heart to tell Janice to mind her own

business. She was only trying to help, Anna knew, but Anna was very uncomfortable with the thought of forcing herself on a man, especially one like Ben. Plus there was still the problem of Lance, who was under the impression that he and Anna were still a couple.

Anna forced her thoughts to return to the church service which was just beginning. She silently gave her problems over to the Lord, confident He would guide her. She hadn't seen Ben yet. The song leader began a hymn, and it wasn't long before Anna lost herself in the beauty of the music. She was so caught up in the uplifting praise she didn't notice when Ben took his place a few rows in front of them.

Ben turned slightly and scanned the auditorium as usual. He smiled at the people who caught his eye. But when he saw Anna standing next to Janice McCray everyone else faded away. He closed his eyes in thanksgiving. Oh, how he had prayed for her last night. Her sadness was a burden on his heart, one he was having trouble understanding, since he barely knew her.

When he opened his eyes, it was to find Anna looking at him, shyness evident in her blushing face. He smiled softly, then turned to walk up the platform steps. He prayed the whole way, for wisdom in dealing with his feelings, and for the strength just to get through the service. He faced the people, and began to worship.

Anna felt her insides quiver when she saw Ben watching her. She had no idea what he was thinking, or for that matter what she was thinking. She was so confused. The only thing she was absolutely positive about was her desire to praise her heavenly Father. She put aside her thoughts of Ben and stepped into worship with the rest of the congregation.

The time passed quickly. Before she realized it, Ben was closing in prayer, and Janice was introducing her to her friends. So much for skipping out as soon as the service was over. "This is Arianna Jenkins," Janice told them. "She's the daughter of Jackie Miller." It seemed as if everyone had known her mother from the kind things they said. Finally, the two women made their way down the aisle, and out into the fresh morning air.

"Janice, Arianna!" someone shouted from behind them. They turned around to see Ben hurrying towards them. "Can I offer to buy you lunch?" he asked breathlessly when he caught up with them.

"That would be wonderful," Janice gushed before Anna could answer. Anna looked askew at her, but Janice smiled innocently. Anna groaned inwardly. She was embarrassed enough as it was and Janice was making it worse by throwing the two of them together.

Ben ignored Arianna's discomfiture and hooked each lady by the arm. They strolled towards downtown. "There's a little diner, not far from here. I eat there often. It's easier than cooking for myself."

Janice snorted. "A home cooked meal is always better for you."

"Is that an invitation?" he asked with a grin.

"You're welcome anytime, Pastor, you know that," she shot back.

Ben laughed. "I know that, Janice. I'm just trying to get a rise out of you."

Anna remained silent, listening to the banter between the two of them. Would she ever feel as comfortable around Ben as Janice obviously did? She was so wrapped up in her thoughts she missed what Ben said to her. "I'm sorry. What did you say?"

"I asked if you enjoyed the service this morning."

Pink ran up Anna's cheeks. "Yes, I did. Very much." She didn't elaborate, but Ben seemed satisfied with her answer. They reached the diner, and conversation was halted while they chose from the menu.

As they waited for their meals to be served, Ben steered the conversation in the direction he wanted. "So Anna, what brought you to church this morning?"

"Don't waste much time, do you, Ben," she complained jokingly. Although she wasn't sure she was ready to share her whole experience with Ben, Anna felt she owed him some explanation, considering he was the one who had started the whole process. "After I left you last night, I realized the truth in your words. It touched something inside me that had been buried for a long time. I guess the Lord decided it was time to get back on the path."

Ben eyes shone. "I'm so glad, Anna," he said softly. "So very glad." He didn't say anything more, but Anna could tell from his look that he had wanted to add something.

The rest of their time together passed quickly. Too quickly for Anna, who was finally beginning to feel at ease in Ben's company. The talk around the table was light and serious in turn. Janice shared with them her wish to travel, although she wasn't certain who would run the hotel. Ben told her that there were any number of willing people around who would help out. Anna seconded that, telling the woman that Anna herself would find it a pleasure to stay there and work.

"You have your own work to do, Anna," Janice declined nicely. "How are you coming with it, by the way?" she asked, deliberately changing the subject to focus on Anna.

Anna took a last sip of her coffee before answering. "To be honest, I don't really know. I got some great shots, but there's so much. I'm going to have a hard time deciding what to include and what to leave out."

The trio rose from their chairs and headed out the door into the bright sunshine. "I'd like to see some of your work," Ben commented, as they walked slowly back to the church.

Anna smiled. "You've already seen some of it."

Ben glanced at her, confusion evident on his face.

"The book on your coffee table. *Soaring Eagles*."

"That's yours?" Ben was astounded. He had seen it in a bookstore several years ago, and had been enchanted by the photographer's ability to capture the true image of animals in nature. Looking through *Soaring Eagles* always brought memories of his time in Montana, and his admiration for God's creation. "I love that book."

"Thank you," Anna laughingly made a half bow. "I must

admit, it's one of my favorites, too. I had such a wonderful time working on it. It was during that time when I first noticed there was something wrong in my life. I just couldn't put my finger on it then."

They came to a stop in front of Janice's sedan. "Will you be here tonight?" Ben asked Anna.

"I'm sorry Ben, I can't. I have to go over to Williamsburg for a few days. My publisher is getting very antsy, so I promised her I would meet with her tomorrow morning," Anna explained. "She'll only be on this side of the country for a few days, and I need to take advantage of it. If I don't I'll have to fly out to L.A., and I don't want to do that right now."

Ben hid his disappointment. He thought it strange he should feel that way, since by his own admission he wasn't planning on pursuing a relationship with her. But he also didn't want her to leave, and was relieved she had decided not to return to California just yet. Forcing his mind back on the conversation at hand he asked, "How are you getting there?"

"Oh, I'll drive over. It's only few hours away. Besides, you never know what pictures are waiting unless you go look for them."

Ben laughed. "That's very philosophical of you."

Anna gave him a haughty look. "I am a very philosophical person." Despite her best attempt Anna couldn't control her giggles.

The look Ben gave her was warm. "I'll just bet you are." He turned serious. "Have a good trip. And be careful, O.K.?" He helped her into Janice's car and shut the door for her.

Anna sensed a hidden meaning behind the words, and answered softly, "I will. Don't worry." Then Janice drove off, leaving Ben waving behind them.

"Our Pastor has quite a soft spot for you," Janice observed quietly.

Anna turned to the woman in surprise. "I don't think so. There's no way a pastor would be interested in someone like me."

It was Janice's turn to look surprised. "What do you mean 'someone like you'? You're a wonderful person, Arianna Jenkins."

"Thanks for the vote of confidence, Janice, but I'm just not stable enough for Ben. Even if he had time for a relationship, which is rather obvious he doesn't, he'd pick a nice mellow woman from the church. Not some person who can't even stay in one place long enough to set roots down."

Janice gave a very unladylike snort. "You don't believe any of that guff you were just saying, do you?"

Anna was very serious. "I'm not right for Ben." She refused to talk about it any more, even though Janice stubbornly tried to pursue the topic. Anna's faith might be restored, but her feelings of inadequacy were still very much present. Her own father wouldn't stay around to love her, and the men she dated only wanted her in their beds. Why would a Godly man like Ben want her to be part of his life?

Totally ignoring the beautiful scenery around her, Anna mentally debated the question all the way to Williamsburg that afternoon. A part of her knew that with God all things were possible. Even a relationship with Ben was possible if God was there. But there was still a part of Anna that couldn't let go of the pain of feeling not good enough, especially not for a man who was as special as she knew Ben to be.

Anna checked into the Holiday Inn, intent on relaxing until the next morning when she was scheduled to meet Lauren Hiller, her publisher. Anna respected the woman and the things she had accomplished in her short life. Lauren was only a year older than Anna's twenty-six, and had built a small, but reputable, publishing house. She was very particular about the items she published, which was why she insisted on meeting with her people in person. That way everyone knew what was expected of them, and Lauren knew exactly what she was getting.

The night passed quietly. Anna's dreams were filled with images of Ben, and she found herself waking early, feeling vaguely unsettled. She gave up on going back to sleep, instead opting to go for an early morning swim. She swam lap after lap in the deserted hotel pool, finally dragging herself out. Anna was practically exhausted as she walked back to her room, but at least her emotions were on a more even keel.

Her appointment with Lauren was set for nine o'clock, at the hotel restaurant.Lauren greeted Anna warmly as she sat down at the table.The two women had a good working relationship that had built up to a great friendship, but with Anna being in Virginia the last month and up in the mountains for months before that, they had not seen much of each other.

"So, how's things, Arianna," Lauren asked.Lauren always referred to Anna by her full name because, she told Anna once, she found it too beautiful to shorten.

Anna launched into an account of how she had spent the past month, excluding her encounters with Ben. If she knew Lauren, and she did, the woman would give her absolutely no peace until every last emotion was analyzed. Being a practical woman, Lauren felt that you should always let the other person know what you were feeling. But because her feelings for Ben were so new, Anna wasn't ready to share them with Lauren.

Anna did tell her friend that she had begun work on a new project that might prove to be one of the best she had to date."I thought I would do a coffee table book on Jordon and the surrounding area in all four seasons. I've got some great shots of the people and a few interesting places. I might even expand on the theme and give it a personal twist."

Lauren sat up straighter, as she always did when serious business was being discussed. She had almost a sixth sense where new projects were concerned, and right now it was quivering madly. "It sounds great so far. I like the personal aspect. I think people would really go for that." Lauren suddenly looked at Anna, as the whole message finally got through. "What do you mean, all four seasons? That's a whole year."

"I've always liked that about you Lauren. You're so quick," Anna laughed.

Lauren stuck out her tongue. "It's still early in the day

for me. You know I'm a night owl. But let's get back to the original conversation, here."

"And that is?"

"You staying here for a whole year."

"So what's wrong with that," Anna wanted to know.

"Not a thing," Lauren replied. "But what is Lance going to say?"

Anna's smile left her face. She had intentionally ignored any thoughts of Lance since they left her with a bad feeling. "I really don't care what he thinks. We didn't exactly part on the best of terms." She didn't want to relate what really happened. Lauren had introduced the two of them in the first place, and Anna didn't want Lauren to feel guilty.

Lauren had no such compunction. "He tried something, didn't he?"

Anna grimaced in distaste. "Something. I managed to ward him off, but there is just no way I can keep on seeing him. He wants more than I am willing to give."

"Stick to your guns, Arianna. I may have introduced you, but I never thought it would progress to serious dating. If I had known that, I never would have introduced you in the first place. He's a lech, and I don't care who hears me. He's only out to satisfy himself, and it doesn't matter who he uses on the way. I'm just glad you found out in time."

"I hope this isn't leading to an 'I told you so'," Anna teased, "even though I deserve one. I should have listened to you, and to my mother. Then I could have avoided this whole mess."

Lauren laughed. "I'll just make it 'better late than never'. Now let's get down to business."

The two women sat over their meals and discussed the layout of Anna's new book. It was decided it should start with spring and work its way through the seasons until it was spring again. Anna had no problem with that. She was looking forward to spending the next year here.

"You still have two assignments that need to be finished in the meantime, you know," Lauren reminded her.

Anna hit her head with her hand. She had totally forgotten. A white water rafting trip brochure and a sequel to *Soaring Eagles* were both in the works. In fact, the rafting trip was scheduled to take place in the next few weeks.

"I assume by the look on your face that it slipped your mind," Lauren commented. "No matter. You still have plenty of time to finish *Whispering Wilds*. How far along are you?"

Business continued as Anna relayed her progress on her current book. They finished their coffees, then sat back to brainstorm on a few more ideas for *Whispering Wilds*. Lauren wanted some things changed, and others added. Nothing Anna thought too difficult. Lauren gave her free reign over most of her assignments, only intervening when she felt it was for the good of the project.

"That's that," Lauren said with satisfaction some three hours later. She closed her notebook with a snap. "Now, my girl, let's get down to some serious business."

A long standing tradition had developed between the two friends. Whenever they got together to discuss business, they would spend at least the same amount of time shopping. It was something they both enjoyed, and it helped to relieve any tension that may have built up between them during their business meeting. At least that's what they told everyone. In truth it was a time for them to relax and be friends in a world where time seemed to be at such a premium.

After leaving the last department store late that afternoon laden with packages, mostly Lauren's, Anna insisted they visit a camping store. "Why are we here?" Lauren questioned, as she watched Anna head towards the tents.

"My tent was blown away during a storm on the mountain a few months ago. Terri and I had to share hers for the last two weeks of the assignment. It was mighty crowded. I haven't been able to replace it yet, and I'm going to need it soon."

Lauren looked confused. "What do you need a tent for?"

Anna frowned at her friend. "Just where do you think I get those pictures, Lauren? Out my bathroom window?"

"Well, no. But I didn't think you actually stayed out in the back of beyond."

Anna had to laugh at Lauren's remark.Her friend's idea of roughing it was the Holiday Inn instead of the Hilton. "There are times when I have to spend a lot of time setting up to get a good shot. It's easier to try to blend in as much as possible. That way the animals get used to me and let their guard down a bit."

"But aren't there, like, bugs and stuff?"

"Yes, Lauren, there are bugs and 'stuff'." She grinned at Lauren's shudder. She would have pressed the advantage and gone on into gory details, but Lauren took matters into her own hands and walked as far away as possible. Half and hour later, purchases made, Anna and Lauren headed back to the hotel to spend what was left of the afternoon and evening lazing around the pool.

Six

On Tuesday morning, Anna made an early start for Jordon. She and Lauren had said their good-byes the previous night at dinner with Lauren assuring Anna she would pass on Anna's intentions of staying in Jordon to Lance. Anna felt sure Lauren would quite enjoy thwarting Lance's advances toward her. She almost felt sorry for Lance, but not sorry enough to try and contact him again, considering the way he sounded the last time they spoke.

The ride was peaceful for the first hour or so. But the closer she got to Jordon the darker the sky became until finally the heavens opened and rain came crashing down. The severe weather made driving extremely hazardous. Anna was having a difficult time keeping the Jeep under control, even with all the off road training she had. She crept along the highway until she reached the outer edge of the town. She was just past Ben's house when the Jeep got away from her and went hurling into a ditch.

Although unhurt, Anna was slightly stunned. It had happened so quickly she hadn't even been able to react. "Drat," she mumbled. Despite the driving course she had taken when she first bought the Jeep, Anna was hesitant to try and maneuver it out of the ditch. She wasn't familiar enough with the terrain to know if she were going in the right direction, and the rain was coming down so hard it was difficult to see. Deciding she would be better off calling for a tow truck, Anna stepped out of the Jeep and dropped into knee deep water. "Whoa," she cried, clutching the bottom of the door.

It seemed that the Jeep had stopped just short of a drop off, and when Anna stepped out she fell right into it. Water swirled around her knees, slowly beginning to rise towards her chest. "Time to get out of here," she said to herself. She didn't want to use the Jeep as leverage, since it was already on precarious ground. Instead she pulled herself up the opposite bank, using the long grass growing there to hoist her body out of the water. When she finally reached the top she was not only totally drenched, but covered in mud.

"Nice outfit," a voice shouted near her ear. Anna's head jerked up.In front of her stood Ben, strong and solid. "Need some help?"

"Oh, no," she yelled. "I thought it would be fun to play in the mud."

Ben grinned. She certainly was a sight to see. Whatever color her jeans had been, they were now muddy brown, as was most of her sweater. Her face was also covered in mud. "Hey! Women pay big bucks for this kind of treatment. You're getting yours for free."

Anna couldn't help herself. She began giggling. "I've always been considered a great bargain shopper," she quipped.

"Well, I hate to end the party, but we really should be getting out of the storm. It's getting worse."

"Worse!" Anna squeaked. Ben took her arm in a strong grip and they fought their way through the wind and rain to Ben's house, which was just beyond a stand of trees. "I didn't think it could get any worse," she commented as they pushed through the back door into the kitchen. They dropped, exhausted, onto the kitchen floor.

"Yeah, worse," Ben told her when they finally caught their breath. "They just issued a tornado warning for the area." He stood up, giving a hand to Anna and pulling her up. "You were lucky I saw you."

"How did you see me?" Anna questioned, looking up into his face. She swore she saw a blush staining his cheeks.

"Ah, I was just looking out the window, checking the weather. I saw the Jeep slide over the edge." He looked deep into her eyes. "I was worried. The ditch gets to be like a roaring river in rain like this."

Anna didn't have to wonder if there was a blush on her

cheeks, she could feel it creeping up her neck and making its way up her face. "Well, thanks for being there. I didn't realize the water was so deep."

They stood in embarrassed silence for a few moments, which was broken by the ringing of a telephone. Ben reached into his coat pocket and took out his cellular phone. "Thompson, here," he said into the receiver. He was quiet, listening to the person on the other end, his face becoming more and more set, until finally he hung up.

"What's wrong?" Anna wanted to know, worried by the look on Ben's face.

"That was Ella, Janice's receptionist. The basement flooded and Janice went to see what was wrong. She fell down the stairs and Ella can't get her out."

Anna jumped into action. "Let's go!"

Ben grabbed her. "Wait. Your Jeep will be better than my truck. We've got to get it out of the ditch."

They hurried back into their wet shoes. Ben threw a raincoat at her which she caught in surprise. "This should keep the worst of it off you," he explained as they went back out into the torrent. The wind had risen greatly, practically blowing Anna off her feet. She made a wild grasp for Ben, who reached back and grabbed her hand as they made a dash for the Jeep.

Ben was able to work the vehicle out of the ditch and back onto the road. He drove into town as fast as he dared, praying the whole time. Janice was very special to him, and he was worried that she might be more injured than Ella was letting on. Anna sat next to him, silent herself, trying in her own small way to pray about the situation.

Soon they were pulling into the hotel's driveway, which was awash in a sea of rainwater. Ella threw open the front door and rushed out. "She's been down there almost an hour. She's stuck fast, and I just don't know what to do." When Ben and Anna made to go inside, Ella caught at them. "You can't get in that way. The door to the basement swung shut and is stuck tighter than a fat man in an innertube."

She guided them around the back, where the outside entrance to the basement was. "I was able to get in this way. I could see she was as well as she could be, and she told me to wait until you showed up." Ella thrust a flashlight into Ben's hands. "I have to get back to the front. Since we're a central location, they've set up a relay station here to help folks out." She hurried away.

Ben and Anna started down the dark stairs, Ben shining the flashlight before them. It was eerie, the way the light bounced off the water. Half way down they began calling and both were relieved to hear Janice's voice answering them.

"What took you so long?" she complained kiddingly, her voice strained.

"We got here as soon as we heard," Ben answered, moving closer to the sound.

"What do you mean, 'we'?"

Anna spoke up. "Ben fished me out of the ditch by his house. It must be his lucky day." She followed carefully behind Ben as they waded through the water to where Janice was hanging on to the stair railing. "You never told me about the indoor swimming pool," Anna teased as she took hold of Janice's arm.

"I'll have to charge you more, now you know," the woman shot back. Her face twisted in pain when Ben reached under the water to touch her leg.

He frowned in concern. "I think it might be broken, Janice," he told her. "How long have you been down here?"

"Half an hour, maybe more. I came down to check out the damage and slipped on the stairs.My leg caught between a couple of the steps when they collapsed. I think it might be trapped by some of the things that were stored under here."

"Hold on to her," he commanded Anna. He waded to the door under the stairs, the water almost reaching his knees. "I think I see what the problem is," he called to them. "There are some bricks down here that fell when the stairs did." The two women heard him moving around. "Try to pull her up, Anna."

With her arms reaching around Janice, Anna pulled with all her might. After a brief struggle, she was able to free her.

"Got her, Ben," Anna yelled. He came out and together they carried the woman to the outside entrance. When they were safely on the steps, Ben carefully lifted her up into his arms and carried her the rest of the way.

Rain was still pouring down as the group hurried to the front of the building. They pushed their way through the door and into the lobby. Laying Janice carefully on one of the couches there, Ben began a preliminary examination of her leg. When he reached the place where the break was, Janice winced in pain. "I guess I was right. It's broken. Ella," he called. The woman hurried over to them. "Can you get me Doc Watson on the phone?"

"The phone's out, Ben."

He handed her his cellular. "Use this. And make sure he gets here pronto. I think she may be suffering from hypothermia as well."

As Ella hurried to do his bidding, Anna rushed into Janice's private apartment to get her a change of clothes. "Why don't you step into the kitchen, Ben. I'll get Janice into something warm before the doctor gets here."

As soon as Ben left, Anna carefully removed the older woman's soaked clothes and, after drying her with a fluffy towel, helped her dress in a pair of sweats.

"Thanks, honey," she said wearily. "All this excitement has left me so tired."

"I know, Janice, but you need to stay awake until the doctor gets here. I'll go grab some blankets , and get you some coffee. She turned to Ella who had just hung up the phone. "How long did the doctor say he'd be?"

"He should be over in just a few minutes," Ella responded. "He was already out on the road."

At that moment Ben came in with a tray filled with coffee and donuts. He set it on the table in front of the couch, and poured out four cups.

"You stinker," Janice said to him. "I was saving those doughnuts."

"For what?" Ben wanted to know. "It's not like you're going to get any guests today. The weather is terrible."

Just as he finished speaking the lobby door blew open and half a dozen people piled into the room.

"I spoke too soon," Ben commented as he helped some of those who had fallen. "What's the problem?" he asked one of the men who had come in.

"The road's washed out," one man said. "We figured this would be the best place to wait."

"Well, Ben, don't just stand there," Janice commanded from her position on the couch. "Go get some more coffee going, and bring the rest of those doughnuts out here."

He looked at the woman in bewilderment. She's a marvel, that's for sure, he thought to himself, as he headed back to the kitchen. He filled the large coffee urn, being a practiced hand at making coffee for large numbers of people. "Being a pastor has some advantages," he said softly.

"Talking to yourself, Ben?" Anna asked from the doorway.

Ben turned around, startled. He hadn't heard her come in. "No one else will," he complained jokingly. "All anyone does is order me around."

"Poor baby," Anna grinned.

"I can tell you're sympathetic. Come here and help me get some snacks ready for those people."

"Now who's doing the ordering?"

The two of them worked silently, side by side, until they had enough food for at least twenty. "I have a feeling there are going to be a few more people showing up soon," Ben advised her. They had been listening to the weather report which proclaimed that the storm would probably get worse before it got better. They loaded trays and took them into the lobby where everyone was gathered.

The doctor had arrived and was examining Janice. "It's a break, all right," he told them as they approached. "I've immobilized it, but we need to get her to the hospital for x-rays and plaster." The man glanced around the room at the number of people gathered there."Do any of those need attention?" he asked Ben.

"I don't think so," Ben answered. "How are you planning on getting Janice to the hospital, Doc?"

"Truthfully, Ben, I have no idea. My van is full of supplies at the moment, trying to keep them dry. You have any suggestions?"

Anna and Ben looked at each other. "The jeep," they said in unison. The doctor looked at them in confusion.

"Anna has a Jeep Wrangler. It might be a little uncomfortable, but it will definitely get through."

Doctor Watson mulled the idea over for a moment. "That just might work." He turned to Anna. "Is there enough room to stretch her leg out fully?"

"Yes. The front passenger seat can be laid back, or she might fit in the back seat if we unload a few things," Anna told him.

They spent the next half hour preparing the Jeep and Janice for the trip to the hospital. Ben would drive her over, then come back to help Anna and Ella at McCray House. "I may need to make a visit or two to check on some of my older parishioners. Is that all right?" he asked Anna.

"Sure. I'm not sure how much gas is left, though."

"I'll fill up while I'm out. George at the gas station will probably know if there's anyone who needs help. If we were living in the middle ages he would be the village crier."

Ben and Doc Watson carried Janice out, with Ella and Anna doing their best to cover them with umbrellas in an attempt to keep the worst of the rain off Janice, who was already too cold. They ran back to the hotel as the men drove off.

"Well, Ella, what do we do now?" Anna wondered, looking around the room at the group gathered. Most were sitting on the floor, since there wasn't enough seating in the lobby.

"How about putting them in guest rooms? I think you're the only guest at the moment, which leaves seven rooms left. I have a feeling this might last awhile."

Between the two of them they managed to get the majority of the people settled. The few who didn't have a room, made themselves comfortable in the lobby. Anna went to the kitchen, rummaging through the cupboards for the makings of a quick meal. Ella stepped in to help, and together they were able to put together a decent dinner.

Just as they finished serving the last person the lights went out. There were several screams from the diners, but Ella calmly lit the candles in the wall sconces. "Pretty handy, huh?" she grinned. "There are lamps in every room. Can you light them, Anna, while I clean up here?"

"Sure, Ella." She took a lighted lantern, and went from room to room, lighting the lamps. She entered her own room last. There was a chill in the air now, since the furnace was not working. She looked longingly at the fireplace, seeing herself sitting in front of a roaring fire, then dismissed the thought as selfish. Then an idea hit her. On a tour of the building when she first arrived, Janice had shown her an old woodburning stove in a room off the lobby. It was set up to heat the whole house, but was seldom used now that there was central heating. If they could get it going, there would be enough heat to warm the house so the people wouldn't be too uncomfortable.

Anna rushed down the stairs. She wasn't familiar with the stove, but would approach Mr. Jones. He and his family had staggered in just as Ben and Janice were leaving. Anna had put them in Janice's apartment since there were seven in the family and Janice's rooms were the only ones big enough to accommodate all of them. He had offered his help if any was needed, so Anna decided to take him up on his offer.

She knocked on the door. "Mr. Jones," she called tentatively.

The door was opened quickly. "Yes, Anna. Is there something I can help you with?" he asked.

"As a matter of fact, yes, there is. I was wondering if you and your boys could help me haul some wood in from the shed out back. I thought if we could get the woodstove going, the guests would have some heat," she explained.

"That's a wonderful idea," he told her. He called his sons, who came running. All five of them. "Miss Anna needs a hand, boys," he told them. "Get your coats on and let's get to work."

The boys threw on their raincoats, pulled on their shoes, and ran through the kitchen and out the back door. They needed no prompting, thinking it great fun to run through the mud and rain and not be scolded. In record time they had brought in enough wood to last through the night. Tim Jones proved to be a whizz with the heater as well, and soon had it going.

With the guests comfortable, Anna and Ella were able to unwind a bit over a cup of coffee in the kitchen. As they were sitting there, it suddenly occurred to Anna that neither of them had checked the water level in the basement in some time. She popped up and tugged on the door until she was finally able to jerk it open. She gasped when she saw the where the water was.

"Ella," Anna said as calmly as she could. "I think we might have a problem." Ella joined her at the door, and both stared down into the basement. The water was swirling, rising almost to the middle of the staircase.

"Oh, heavens," Ella whispered.

Anna turned to her. "We've got to do something, Ella. Is there any way to pump it out?"

"Oh, shoot," Ella moaned.

"What's wrong?"

"I totally forgot about the pump. It works off electricity. When we lost power I wasn't thinking about the water in the basement. We've got to get the pump going somehow."

Once again, Anna found herself running to Tim Jones, who was happy to help. "I saw an old generator in the shed when we were hauling in the wood. I'm not an electrician or anything, but I'm fairly good at rigging things to keep them going until the repair man can get there." He called his oldest son, and the two of them went out to the shed to check out the generator.

They set the machine up on the back patio, and Tim set to

work. Within half an hour they had the generator running. "Now, I just have to figure out how to get the pump hooked up," he told the women. The water was almost up to the last step when he shouted, "Eureka!" With the flip of a switch the pump came to life and they watched the water slowly back off.

"You're a life saver, Tim," Anna told him.

"I never could have done it without the Lord's help," he commented. "I haven't prayed so hard since Jamie broke his leg last winter."

Anna smiled, thinking that she had never prayed so hard period. With the pump working, and the guests taken care of, Anna and Ella were finally able to retire to their own rooms for the night. Anna started a fire in the grate, then fell exhausted into a chair. Her thoughts were troubled. She was afraid for Ben, who was traveling around in this mess, trying to lighten the worries of some of his congregation.

Who would have thought, Anna smiled wearily to herself, that I would find myself attracted to a pastor, especially considering the last man I dated. Thoughts of Lance sobered Anna instantly. She was still worried about those phone calls she had received. Lance was acting very strange, even for him. Anna pushed those thoughts from her mind, instead trying to focus on what she needed to be doing. Praying.

Seven

Ben stood at the door and stared at the sleeping woman, his heart beating a tattoo in his chest. She was so beautiful, her feet drawn up under her, her head resting on the back of the chair. Her coppery hair fell in wild waves, framing her pale face. He hated to wake her, but had no choice.

"Arianna," he called softly. She didn't stir, so he quietly approached the chair. He gently laid his hand on her arm. "Arianna," he repeated, shaking her slightly.

Anna came slowly awake, a pleasant warmth enveloping her. She opened her eyes and found herself staring into soft gray ones. It registered slowly that Ben was leaning over her, trying to wake her, but she was reluctant to let go of sleep. She had been having the most wonderful dream about her and Ben.

"Hi, sleepy head," he laughed softly. Her chocolate brown eyes were having trouble focusing on him. He wanted so much to reach down and kiss her he had to force himself to stand up and away from her. Their friendship was tenuous at best, and he didn't want to risk it by acting with his hormones. So instead of kissing her, he held out his hand. She took it and he pulled her gently to her feet.

"Sorry to wake you," Ben apologized, "but Janice is downstairs, and could use some help."

Anna became fully awake. She had almost forgotten about Janice's broken leg. "Is she well enough to be here?"

"The doc seemed to think she would be better off here. The storm's over and most of the people have already left."

"Already gone?" Anna questioned. "What time is it?"

Ben laughed. "It's almost ten-thirty."

Anna's mouth opened in astonishment. "Ten-thirty! Why did you let me sleep so late?" she accused him, as she pushed him towards the door. "Tell Janice I'll be down in ten minutes. I hope you didn't send those people away without something to eat," she warned him as she closed the door in his face.

Ben stood there, not sure whether to break out laughing or be upset that she had practically shoved him out of her room. Well, it is her room, he told himself as he turned toward the stairs. He delivered Arianna's message to Janice, then left to continue his own work.

Anna came running downstairs some ten minutes later, her wet hair drawn into a tight braid hanging down her back. She flew into Janice's apartment to find the woman comfortably entrenched on her sofa, with half a dozen novels lying on the coffee table next to her. She looked up as Anna came hurrying in, a smile lighting her face.

"I'm sorry to have slept so late," Anna apologized, as she sat on the edge of the table. "Is there anything you need?"

Janice laughed. "I'm just fine, dear. As you can see, I shall be busy for quite awhile." She motioned to the books. "Ella brought me some reading material." She laughed again. "I'd have to be in bed for a year to be able to read all those."

Anna reached for the woman's hand. "I'm just glad there's nothing seriously wrong."

"I am too," Janice admitted. "I have to admit I was scared yesterday. But the doc assures me I should be back on my feet in less than six weeks, which is good considering how bad the break was. My only worry is the hotel. With summer coming business will pick up considerably. I have no idea how I'll be able to manage."

Anna gave Janice an assessing glance. Janice was known for her optimism, which was at odds with her words. She stared at the woman in silence, then detected a gleam in the other woman's eyes that definitely belied her serious words. What a conniver, Anna thought with a silent chuckle. Let's see if we can get her goat.

"Oh, Janice, that's too bad. I guess you'll just have to shut the place down until you're back on your feet."

Janice's head shot up. She glared at Anna, who had

turned away from her. It wasn't until Anna turned around that Janice realized she had been had. Anna's brown eyes were twinkling merrily, and she couldn't contain her grin. "Serves you right," Anna said. "You know I would be happy to help you in any way I can."

The two women spent the next hour discussing just how Anna could help, and how to go about doing it. With notes in hand, Anna headed for the reception desk, ready to tackle some of the computer entry work that needed to be finished. Ella arrived a short while later, and the two of them together were able to sort out the supplies that would be needed in the next few weeks. Janice had booked a small group who were due to arrive the following week, and she still needed to prepare for them.

After three hours at the computer, Anna's neck and back were aching. She decided a break was just what she needed. Leaving Janice and the hotel in Ella's capable hands, she left the hotel, camera in hand. The storm had done a great deal of damage, but already people were working on repairs. Anna snapped pictures of citizens picking up around town, as well as shopkeepers and homeowners cleaning up. She fought the desire to hop in her Jeep and go out to Ben's. Although she was attracted to him, she didn't think it would look right for her to just appear at his home without an invitation.

So instead she walked through town and trudged up the hill to the ridge. She was drawn to this place both because of its rugged beauty and the fact that she had first met Ben here. Anna peered over the edge, watching the swollen river raging below. The previous day's heavy rain had caused the river to rise a great deal, causing the flood in town and the white water below. The contrast between the gentle river she was accustom to and the one she was now seeing was amazing.

Anna took several pictures, then sat under a tree a short distance away. Ideas for her book flitted through her head. She pulled her notebook out of her camera bag, and began writing furiously so as not to lose the thread of her thoughts. When she read back through them, she was quite pleased with what she had written. Just what Lauren wants, Anna told herself. She jumped up and walked back to the hotel, whistling happily.

"Where have you been?" Ella demanded when Anna entered the lobby.

Anna looked at her in surprise. Ella was normally a very soft spoken person. "I walked around town and took some pictures, then went up to the ridge," she told the woman. "Why?"

Ella didn't say anything, just looked at her. Anna had no idea what was going on, and was just about to ask, when Ben appeared from the kitchen.

"Where have you been?" he practically shouted.

Anna stepped back in surprise. Ben's voice had a hard edge to it, one she had never heard before. "I took a walk around town," she explained, trying to keep the tremble out of her voice. She would have gone on, but Ben wheeled around and left the room. Anna looked at Ella in confusion, but she had also turned away. Hurt and slightly angry, Anna went to her room and locked the door. The tears she had held in check fell steadily down her cheeks. She threw herself on her bed, burying her head in her pillow to muffle her sobs.

It was some time later when Ben knocked on Arianna's door. He had been too angry when Anna had come back to speak with her concerning the phone call he had taken during her absence. A man claiming to be Anna's fiancee had phoned and left a very intimate message for her. Ben had held his temper in check, but it had finally exploded when he saw her. He had tried to ignore the confusion and pain in her eyes. Knowing that his behavior displeased God, he decided he would apologize then leave and not see her again.

He knocked, then waited. When, after a few more knocks there was still no answer, Ben grew worried. Taking the pass key from his pocket, he quietly unlocked the door and peered inside the dim room. Anna was lying on the bed, hugging her pillow, fast asleep. Traces of tears were evident, making Ben feel like a total heel. He didn't have the heart to wake her, and silently left the room.

Before leaving the hotel, Ben went to talk to Janice. She had been resting earlier, and not wanting to bother her, Ben had not sought her advice about Anna's phone call. A decision he had cause to regret after speaking to her.

"Oh, Ben," Janice sighed heavily.

"What do you mean, 'oh Ben'. Why didn't she tell me she was engaged?" Ben couldn't conceal the anger in his voice.

Janice looked at him, brows raised. "Did you ever ask her if she were seeing anyone?" she questioned.

"No," he admitted. "She mentioned some man named Lance, but only said something about him reminding her mother of her father."

"Did you ask the name of the man who called? Did he say what his name was?" Janice asked.

"Well, no," Ben mumbled.

Although Janice smiled, her voice was serious. "I can only assume it's the Lance person Anna spoke about. He's called Anna several times since she's been here. Mostly during the last week. From what Arianna has told me he's been rather, shall we say adamant, about her returning to California. She also told me that she has no intention of continuing the relationship." Janice gave him a level stare. "I don't believe she would lie to me about it, and I don't believe she has ever lied to you."

"Janice, what am I suppose to do? I really blew it. I'm suppose to be a shepherd of people, not their judge."

"We all make mistakes, Ben, even pastors. But the Bible says don't let the sun go down on your anger. You're running out of time," she said, nodding to the window where they could see the sun sinking below the mountains.

Ben smiled. He used that verse often when counseling couples with problems. When he thought about it, this reminded him of his other counseling sessions, only he was a participant this time. I definitely don't want to make a habit out of this, he thought as he went back upstairs. He knocked boldly on Anna's door, and was rewarded by a mumbled 'come in'. Arianna sat in her chair facing the empty fireplace, head resting on her upraised knees. She looked up when Ben entered, and Ben saw tears on her cheeks. Unable to find the words to say, he moved, sweeping her up into his arms and holding her tight as her sobs increased. He cradled her against his chest, sitting down in the chair he had taken her out of.

"What did I do?" she hiccuped, when the worst was over.

Ben's heart tore in pain. "Oh, Arianna, it wasn't anything you did," he assured her, holding her even tighter. "It was me. It was jealousy, plain and simple."

Anna pulled back and looked up into Ben's face, confusion in her eyes. "Jealous? Why?" Then, "Of who?"

Ben took a deep gulp of breath before he answered. "Let me answer the who first. A man called this afternoon while you were out. He didn't give his name, and fool that I am, I didn't ask. He said he was your fiancee." Ben paused a moment. "He also said a few other things." He watched Arianna's face grow pale.

"What other things," she whispered.

"Arianna, he said things that only someone with intimate knowledge of another person would say." Ben paused, waiting for Anna's response. She grew even more pale, if that were possible. Ben thought for a moment she might faint. Her face was white as a sheet.

He was wrong. Anna sprang out of his lap, back rigid in fury. In all her years Anna had never known such anger. Lance was the only person who had her number other than Lauren. He had to be the one who called earlier. Exactly what he said or why he did it Anna had no idea, but when she spoke to him about it, which she intended to do immediately, she would let him know in no uncertain terms that she would absolutely not see him again.

From his vantage point in the chair, Ben watched as Anna paced back and forth in front of her balcony door. It didn't take a rocket scientist to tell she was angry. No, angry was not the right word. Explosive would be more appropriate. Hopefully not directed at me, he thought ruefully. While he watched her pace, he couldn't help noticing how positively gorgeous she was. Her brown eyes were almost black, and her cheeks were now flushed a deep pink. As she marched from end to end, her coppery braid swinging behind her, she looked like an avenging angel. Before his thoughts got away from him Ben knew he had to do something.

"Anna," he said, rising from the chair. "I know you're angry at this person..."

"How do you know it's Lance I'm angry with?"she tossed at him. Before he answered, she once again turned her back on him to gaze out the window.

Ben came to stand behind her. He knew he deserved that. He had never even told her why he was angry. The call had just been such a surprise, and Janice's revelation about Arianna's previous calls really had him feeling like a heel.

He had a desperate desire to touch her, to feel her warmth again. He placed his hands gently on her shoulders, ignoring her stiffness. "I'm sorry Arianna. Please forgive me."

Anna turned her head so she could look into his face. Ben's gray eyes were sober in the dim light, somber and filled with remorse. She looked back outside. "I'm sorry too."

Ben gently began to rub the tension from her shoulders. "Arianna," he said while continuing to massage her neck. "I know you don't want to hear this, but you need to forgive whoever it was who called." Anna grew perfectly still under his hands. "You've made a wonderful step of commitment while you've been here. Don't let the foolish actions of another person steal your joy."

Ben could tell Anna was mulling over his words. Her body slumped from the burden of her anger. Ben turned her to face him, taking her unresisting body in his arms, giving her the comfort and support she needed.

Anna knew the wisdom of Ben's words. Her losing her temper was not the solution to her problem with Lance. But she also realized that until she resolved the dilemma, any relationship with Ben could not go forward. That caused her a moment of pain, but also joy. For the first time in her life, she felt the faint stirrings of true love, and praised God for it.

Straightening up, Anna stepped out of Ben's embrace, and looked directly in his eyes. "I know that I have to, Ben, but it's not going to be easy. I guess I need to explain my relationship with Lance." She motioned to Ben to be seated. Anna began pacing again. "My publisher, Lauren Hiller, introduced us some time ago. When he asked me out I was flattered. He's goodlooking and famous, and I guess I got caught up in that. But I knew almost from the beginning that we weren't right for each other.

"The nature of both of our jobs makes us both travel a lot. Between jobs we saw quite a bit of each other. It didn't take Lance long to ask me to bed," a blush spread over her cheeks as Anna said the words. "I refused, telling him I was waiting for marriage. He seemed to accept it, but never stopped asking. I overheard a conversation one night at a party we were attending, and confronted Lance. Let's just say he didn't take my last refusal very well."

Ben could feel the anger rising in him. He could imagine what happened, and wanted very much to punch this Lance person's lights out. But, a voice inside him reasoned, it's not your problem. You don't have time for a relationship, remember? He looked up at Arianna who was standing in front of him. Who am I trying to kid, he thought.

Anna smiled when she looked into Ben's face. In his eyes she recognized the same confusion she saw in her own eyes lately when she looked in the mirror. He was struggling with his feelings as much as she was struggling with her own. "I know what I have to do," she said again. "I intend to break totally with Lance, and since he hasn't listened to me long distance, I'll have to go back and face him directly."

Ben's startled eyes met Anna's. In hers he saw grim determination, and something else he couldn't define. He stood, and noticed, not for the first time, how fragile she appeared. But he knew that underneath that delicate appearance was a strength now made even more resilient by her faith.

He reached out and took her hands in his, looking deep

into those chocolate brown eyes. Ben knew he didn't have a right to, but it was like trying to stop the sea from washing up on the shore. He lowered his head and brushed his lips over hers. The kiss was soft and sweet and Ben thought he might die from the heart palpitations it was giving him.

Anna was affected strongly as well, so much so that her legs began to tremble. Her eyes closed and she let the sweetness of the kiss wash over her. When she opened her eyes, Ben was staring at her, a strange light in his eyes. They stood there gazing at each other, until the ringing of the phone caused them both to jump.

Anna was slow to answer, fearing it might be Lance. Ben made to pick it up but she forestalled him. "I'll get it, Ben," she told him softly. She reached over, lifting the receiver like it might bite her. "Hello."

Lauren's voice came over the line. "Am I glad I caught you," she said.

Anna let out the breath she had been holding. "What's up, Lauren?" she asked, motioning to let Ben know it was all right. He gestured silently with his head that he would leave, but Anna held up her hand to stop him.

"I talked to Lance yesterday, Arianna," Lauren said. "He was absolutely furious."Lauren went on to say that Lance's anger was totally out of proportion. "I can't figure it out."

"What exactly did you tell him," Anna queried.

"I told him you had decided to stay out east to work. Nothing else."

"You didn't hint that maybe I had met someone else, did you?"

"Well, not exactly," Lauren's voice held a tinge of guilt.

Anna moaned. "Lauren, how could you do that? I never said I was seeing anyone here." At that comment Ben's ears perked up. If he was quiet he might learn something about how Arianna felt towards him. "He called here earlier today, and left a rather explicit message with a friend of mine." Ben wasn't sure he liked the sound of that. He didn't want to be a 'friend'. Anna was silent for a minute while she listened to this Lauren person on the other end. "I'll have to come there."

"He isn't here," Lauren told her.

"What do you mean he isn't there. He just called a few hours ago."

"I talked to Pete just before I called you. After his call to you Lance stormed off the set, and no one knows where he went."

Arianna was silent. "All right. I'll hang out here for awhile longer, but I have to talk to him." She and Lauren chatted a few minutes longer than Anna hung up the phone. She turned to face Ben who was sitting in the chair in front of the fireplace. "That was Lauren," she explained unnecessarily.

Ben stood. "I heard." They stared at each other for another minute. "Arianna," Ben began. "I know we haven't known each other very long, and this probably isn't the best time to ask, but I would like to get to know you better," he went on. "Please, don't leave yet."

Anna smiled. "There doesn't seem to be any point going at the moment. Lance isn't there."

"How about dinner tomorrow?" Ben burst out.

She couldn't contain her grin. She found it funny that two grown adults could be so nervous. "I'd love to, Ben."

Eight

Anna looked forward to dinner with anticipation. This would be her first 'real' date with Ben, since she didn't count the dinner they had at the Flower Shop as a date. She was excited and nervous. Several times during the day she glanced over at the clock, bemoaning how slow time was passing.

Janice watched Arianna flutter around her apartment, amusement evident on her face. Anna reminded her of a teenager going on her first date. She wondered how Ben was faring, then chuckled. If she knew Ben he was as nervous as Arianna. "So where are you going, dear?" Janice asked, hoping to ease Anna's jitters.

"I don't know," Anna answered. "He told me to wear my white dress, but to bring some jeans and my hiking boots." The younger woman roamed through Janice's sitting room, seeming like a caged animal.

"Why don't you take a walk or something," Janice suggested. Anna turned to look at her. "You're pacing like a wild animal stuck in a cage. It pains me to see you like this."

Anna laughed. "I'm being silly, aren't I?"

Janice smiled. "Not silly, child. Normal. A walk will do you good. Take Hetty. She hasn't been out for long a walk since my accident."

Anna took Janice's advice. She and Hetty strolled around town, greeting and being greeted by the people they met along the way. It helped to take her mind off her date with Ben, and gave her a few ideas about the pictures she would take this summer. By the time they returned to McCray House it was time for Anna to prepare for the big event.

Ben was waiting at the bottom of the stairs when Arianna came down. The white dress swirled around her ankles, making her look like an angel to Ben. Her auburn hair was loose, hanging down to her waist in softly flowing ripples. His heart constricted in his chest. She was so absolutely beautiful, and she was his for the evening.

Anna's eyes smiled when they met Ben's. Without a word he took her hand when she reached the bottom step. Still a few inches taller than her, despite the step she stood on, Ben bent his head and kissed her softly on the cheek. "You are positively ravishing, my dear," his whispered southern drawl tickling her ear. The blush that spread over her cheeks enchanted Ben, making him want to say something equally outrageous just to see the lovely color. He resisted, instead leading her through the lobby to Janice's apartment. "She wants to say good-night," he explained.

They make a striking couple, Janice thought to herself as she watched the two coming towards her. "Have a good time, dear," she told Anna when the younger woman bent down to kiss her cheek. "And behave yourself," she warned Ben, who just smiled.

"Don't wait up," he tossed over his shoulder as he and Anna departed. "Do you mind if we take your Jeep?" Ben asked as they walked out to the car park.

"No, not at all." Ben handed her into the passenger seat, then jumped in behind the wheel. He drove through town, getting on the highway to Williamsburg. "Where are we going?" she inquired.

Ben turned his head and smiled. "You'll see," was all he would tell her. Half an hour later he turned into a small parking lot. He parked the Jeep, then came around to help Anna out. Without a word he lead her through the trees at the far end of the lot. There was a brick path, which they followed for a short time. When they reached the end Anna gasped in amazement. There in front of her was the most beautiful home she had ever seen.

"Here we are," Ben said, leading her to the front door.

"What is this place?" Anna whispered in awe.

Ben grinned. "I found it one night on my way back from Williamsburg. It's a gourmet restaurant. They take reservations for only ten couples a night. I was lucky to get reservations so easily." Ben opened the heavy wooden door and they entered the building.

They stood in the foyer, marble tiles underfoot and a glistening chandelier overhead. Anna gazed around her in wonder. One wall of the foyer was covered with a huge tapestry depicting a scene reminiscent of King Arthur's Knights of the Round Table. The other walls were covered with natural wood paneling, bringing out the beautiful hues of the tapestry.

As a tuxedo clad waiter led them to their table, Anna admired the paintings on the walls, showing scenes from times gone by. Even after they were seated, Anna continued to gaze about her in wonder. The room where they were seated was furnished entirely of antiques, and from what she had seen of the other rooms, they were as well. Their room held two other tables, set a discreet distance from each other to ensure the privacy of the diners. A couch set apart from the tables faced a huge fireplace, where a fire burned merrily.

"This is absolutely beautiful, Ben," Anna told him, her voice filled with admiration.

"Isn't it, though. I was lucky to have found it. They're so far off the beaten track that usually they get their customers only by word of mouth. "He looked very pleased with himself, and Anna had to laugh. "What's so funny?" Ben asked, confusion on his face. This made Anna laugh even harder.

"I'm sorry, Ben," she apologized, when she could speak again. "You looked like a kid who just sneaked a cookie out of the cookie jar. It's so cute." Anna chuckled at the memory.

"Cute, huh?" Ben groused good naturedly. "I don't think I like the idea of being thought of as cute. Terribly handsome, maybe." He gave Anna a saucy grin, and she laughed again.

After the waiter took their order, Ben and Arianna began talking. Conversation flowed easily from one topic to another, as the couple devoured the most delicious meal Anna had had in ages. Ben ordered for both of them, choosing prime rib roasted to perfection. The salad that accompanied the meal was topped with the house's private dressing, a creamy, tangy version of Italian. Along with their main dish came a sparkling cider, which Ben used to toast their new friendship.

At the end of the meal, Ben sat back with a sigh of pleasure. Anna laughed at the contented look on his face. "The way to a man's heart is through his stomach, I'm told," Anna said, a smile on her face. She looked at Ben with a teasing glance. "We are going to order dessert, aren't we?" she questioned innocently.

Ben groaned. "You can't possibly have any room left. I know I'm stuffed to the gills."

"Ah. Is that what I see coming out of your ears," Anna teased.

"Funny. Seriously though. Do you want dessert?"

"I was just kidding. I'm full myself."

Ben looked relieved. "That's good. We'll let our food digest for a bit in the drawing room, then we're going on a little hike. You brought a change of clothes, right?" Ben asked, as he led Anna to the small sofa in front of the fireplace.

Anna looked over her shoulder at him. "Yes, I did, but where are we going?"

"If I told you it wouldn't be a surprise. Do you have your camera, by chance?"

"Actually, yes I do. I put it in the car this morning when I thought I was going to snap a few pictures around town. But Janice needed me and I didn't get a chance."

"Perfect," Ben commented. "I'll run out to the Jeep and get the clothes." He left, returning a few minutes later. He handed Anna her duffle bag containing her jeans, sweater, and hiking boots, then sat down next to her. "It'll be easier to change here," he informed Anna. "So how do you like our little town?" Ben inquired, changing the subject.

Anna thought about it for a moment before answering. "I like it. It isn't what I expected when I told my mom I would come. I've lived in the big city my whole life, and even though I thoroughly enjoy my time in the wilderness, I've always liked my city life. But the more time I spend here, the more I realize how empty my life really was. I guess my mom was smarter than I gave her credit for."

Ben gave her a compassionate look. "I can relate to that. When my mom sent me to live with my grandparents in Montana, I thought she was crazy. Even though life was becoming unbearable here, I didn't want to leave, especially without my mom. It was all I knew. But she sent me anyway. And I came to love my life in Montana.

"When my mom died, we came back for the funeral. It didn't feel like home anymore. But when I came back as an adult, everything fit. It was home again."

"Do you miss your grandparents?" Anna questioned. She was curious about Ben's family. He was such a wonderful person, she couldn't perceive his family being any different. His mother loved him so much she sacrificed her time with him to make sure he would be happy. Anna respected that. Her mother had been the same way.

"Yes, I miss them very much," Ben interrupted her thoughts. "They're coming out this summer. Gramps promised to help me get the house and barn in order. He's great at handy work, and now that he's retired full-time, he and Gramma promised to come."

Anna tried to work out the numbers in her head, but she had to ask, "How old are they?"

Ben laughed. "They're in their seventies. They had mom really young. Gramma was only sixteen when they got married. I tease them about that, because when I was sixteen they were hesitant to even let me date. Mom was born a year later. She married when she was twenty, against my grandparents wishes. My dad was killed in a brawl at a bar, but mom wouldn't go back to Montana. She was too proud. So I grew up here. My dad's reputation wasn't very good, so my mom had kind of a hard time. I didn't help things any by being such a mischievous kid. But mom always loved me." Ben's eyes were soft with remembrance.

A moment later he was jumping up off the couch,

grabbing Anna's hand, and urging her to the ladies room to change her clothes. They met in the lobby, then walked out to the Jeep. He handed her in, then started the engine, and drove back towards Jordon.

They were silent, but when they drove through town, Anna glanced curiously at her companion. He had a secretive smile on his face, and if Anna didn't know better she would have thought he was up to something.

Ben felt her eyes on him, and his smile grew wider. He hadn't been this excited since he moved to Jordon. It was obvious from the look on her face that Arianna hadn't a clue as to where they were going, which was probably just as well. If she knew he was going to take her Jeep places where it probably hadn't been before, she might call a halt to the outing, or at least not let him drive, both options equally unsatisfactory to him. So he kept on going, silent, but smiling.

When he drove off the road and onto a small, rough track, Anna let out a gasp. "Where are we going?" she demanded, hanging on for dear life. They were bumping along the track, gradually moving up in altitude.

"There's a very special place I want to show you," Ben replied. After that they didn't speak, mostly because the bumps made it close to impossible."Here we are," Ben remarked, pulling the Jeep into a lie in at the end of the makeshift road.

Ben came around and opened her door. Anna peered into the wilderness, but surrounded as they were by trees, she couldn't make out where they were in relation to Jordon. Ben reached behind her, and pulled out the knapsack sitting on the back seat. He tossed it over his shoulders then motioned for her to follow him. The going was easy at first, but Anna was thankful for her hiking boots after a short time.

Anna wasn't sure where they were going, but she could appreciate the beauty surrounding her. The full moon lighted their way, waving shadows in front and behind them. Ben turned a few times to offer a hand, but Anna was quite capable of fending for herself. In fact she was so happy to be in the wilderness again, she was almost willing to forgive Ben for the torture he put her poor Jeep through.

After hiking for half an hour, Ben came to a stop. Anna halted behind him, glancing around. They were on the top of a ledge jutting out over the fast flowing river below them. Above them, the mountain lay shrouded in an eerie light from the full moon. Anna gasped at the beauty of the picture she was seeing. "Ben, this is beautiful," she whispered. She grasped his arm.

"I think so," he responded. He covered her hand with his. "I came here once when I was ten. Pastor Williams brought me. He told me this was where he came when he wanted to be really close to God. When I moved back to Jordon as pastor, this was the first place I came. Pastor Williams was right. I do feel close to God here."

Ben took a blanket out of the knapsack and spread it out on the flat rock. They sat down and stared up into the heavens. "You can see so much from up here," Anna commented, looking around her. In the distance, the lights of Jordon were just visible. Below them, the river that flowed so sweetly through town, roared.

Ben studied Anna's face as she took in the view. "You sure can," he said, gazing at her.

Something in his tone made Anna glance over at him. There was that strange light in his eyes again. "What did I say?"

"Nothing," he assured her, but kept watching. "I brought a treat," he said, taking pity on her uneasiness. He pulled a covered plastic bowl full of strawberries out of the knapsack, followed by a bottle of sparkling cider and two wine glasses.

"My goodness," Anna marveled. "How did you manage all this?"

Ben grinned. "I refuse to divulge any secrets." He poured the cider into the glasses and handed her one. "A toast," he said. "To getting to know each other." They clinked glasses and drank the sweet drink. When they had finished the toast, Ben continued. "Now, about getting to know each other. You've told me a little bit about yourself, now tell me some more."

"Well," she hesitated, "what exactly do you want to know?"

He considered her question for a moment. He was fairly sure she didn't want to talk about anything too personal. "Tell me about your work. I've seen *Soaring Eagles*. What else have you done, or are you doing?"

Anna happily complied. She loved her work, and enjoyed talking about it. She grinned before she started. Ben didn't know what he was letting himself in for. "I do mostly nature work, but I do the occasional wedding, mostly for friends. There's a sequel, I guess you would call it, to *Soaring Eagles*, called *Whispering Wilds*. I have a few more shoots to do for it, but I've convinced Lauren that I can do them here. The mountains will be a perfect backdrop for what I have planned for the end of the book."

"And what might that be?" Ben wanted to know.

"Now that would be telling," Anna laughed.

They sat there for almost an hour, soaking in the atmosphere. Ben slid closer, drawing her within his embrace. She leaned her head on his shoulder, and he gently rested his head on her hair. It was a long time before either of them spoke.

"Arianna," Ben whispered.

"Yes, Ben?" she whispered back.

"Are you going to stay here?"

"I would like to."

"For how long?"

"For a long time, I hope."

He seemed satisfied with her answer.

A short time later, Ben reluctantly rose, drawing Anna with him. As much as he hated to go, he knew he had a long day tomorrow, and it was very late. But before they began the trek back to the Jeep, Ben knew he was going to kiss her. He drew her gently to him, surrounding her in his muscular arms.

Anna knew what was coming, and she wanted it with all her heart. Ben had become very special to her, even after such a short time. She hesitated to say she was in love with him, but knew that her feelings were strong, and that they weren't going to go away.

Ben lowered his head and brushed her lips with his. It was a light kiss, reverent in its touch, but electrifying just the same. He opened his eyes and looked down at the woman resting against him, as if seeing her for the first time. He had never felt this way about a woman in his life. It was frightening, yet exhilarating at the same time.

Wanting to feel her closeness again, Ben tightened his embrace, and kissed her again. Anna responded to his caress, knowing she was lost. This man she had only know for a few short weeks, held her heart in his hand. The intensity of her feelings frightened her, but she was determined to trust that God would show her the right path.

The kiss deepened, and Anna found herself drifting on a swirl of emotions. She had never been affected by a kiss this way, and it felt wonderful. She slid her hands up Ben's arms, and wound them around his neck, knowing that if she let go she would fall, her legs were so weak. Her fingers twined in his blond hair, enjoying its softness.

Ben groaned in pleasure. But he knew he had to stop. If he didn't stop now he wasn't sure he would be able to. He gently broke the kiss, then rested his head on her soft, auburn hair. "Arianna, you are so beautiful," his breathed. He could feel her shiver, and smiled to himself. At least she wasn't totally unaffected. He cupped her face in his hands, and kissed her mouth again. "I have to stop doing this," he said softly, as he bent his head and once more kissed her.

Anna smiled. She also knew they should stop, but she was enjoying it very much. When he kissed her for the third time, she couldn't hold back a giggle.

Ben looked down at her and laughed. "You drive me crazy woman!" He let her go, and the two of them gathered up their impromptu picnic. As they walked to the trail, Ben put a restraining hand on Anna's arm. She turned to him questioningly. "I wanted you to know that I had a wonderful time tonight."

"I did too, Ben," she replied, smiling up at him.

Her smile sent his heart racing. As much as he wanted to

deny it, he was afraid he was falling hard for this woman, and that wasn't in his plans. He brushed the thought away, and took her hand, leading the way down the trail to the Jeep. The ride home was made in companionable silence, both of them caught up in their own thoughts. When Ben dropped her and the Jeep at the hotel, he gave her one more quick kiss, and left with a mumbled good-night.

Nine

Anna woke the next morning, happy and content. Before falling into bed the night before, she had spent a long time in prayer, asking the Lord for direction in her relationship with Ben. Although there had been no lightning bolt from the blue, she was certain the Lord wasn't disapproving of the time she and Ben were spending together. Perhaps they would spend the rest of their lives together, or perhaps not, but she wasn't worried. Right now she felt they were doing the right thing by getting to know each other.

She stretched lazily and glanced over at the clock. She was astounded to see that it was almost ten o'clock. This is becoming a habit, she grinned to herself, thinking of the morning after the storm. Anna jumped up, and padded to the bathroom. After letting the refreshing water of the shower wash over her, she was ready to begin another day.

Across town, Ben had begun his day hours earlier. He slept poorly last night, dreaming of the kisses they had shared. Even now his heart pounded when he thought of them. Thoughts of Arianna Jenkins intruded on everything he tried to do. He drew his arm across his face, wiping sweat off his brow. Not even the mind numbing monotony of chopping wood had been able to dispel the image of Anna from his mind.

"This is ridiculous," he mumbled out loud. If he didn't get his mind off Arianna and on his work soon, he would accomplish absolutely nothing today. "Maybe I'll head into the office," Ben told himself. Twenty minutes later, his truck was headed toward the church.

He drove past the hotel on his way, his eyes of their own accord searching out Anna's Jeep. It was still in the lot. He let a breath of relief. He was hoping he wasn't the only one affected by their date last night. Then again, Ben thought, Arianna might have just looked on it as passing time. Who are you kidding, he told himself. Unless she was one terrific actress, there was no mistaking her reaction last night. That thought caused a huge smile to spread across his face as he pulled into the church parking lot.

After a concentrated effort, Ben finally managed to get his head into his work, and had been doing it steadily for several hours, when Anna strolled nonchalantly over to the church. Standing at the lobby window earlier she had seen him drive by, and decided she would just mosey by the church, using the excuse that she wanted some photos of it. If she were being truthful, she would admit that she just wanted to see him again. His kisses from the previous night were still giving her shivers. But Anna didn't want to examine the truth just yet.

Anna, feeling guilty about interrupting Ben, took several pictures of the church. It was an old building, made of stone, with a bell in the steeple, and it made a beautiful backdrop for the myriad of colorful flowers planted in front of it. Ben's office was located at the back, where several rooms had been added on. There was a separate entrance to his office which allowed him access to his work whenever he wanted without interrupting anything that might be happening in the sanctuary.

After snapping a few shots of the bell with the brilliant blue sky behind it, Anna tapped softly on Ben's office door. At his muffled 'come in' she quietly opened the door, and entered the room. She had never seen his office before, and was impressed both by the tasteful decor, and the large number of books on the shelves. Being an avid reader, she had a fondness for books, old or new, and was always interested in finding new reading material.

Ben looked up when the door opened, and smiled broadly when he saw Arianna standing just inside. She looked delightfully nervous, just how he felt. He leaned back in his chair, striving to look casual even though his heart was beating so hard he thought it might jump right out of his chest. "What can I do for you, Arianna?" he asked.

Anna hesitated. I've got to think of some excuse for being here, she berated herself. Ah, I've got it. "I can't seem to find my keys," she told him. "You wouldn't happen to have them, would you?" It wasn't a lie, exactly. She knew he had them, since she had seen him put them in his jeans pocket last night when he walked her to the door.

Ben thought a moment, trying to remember. His head had been so muddled last night he could barely remember his own name, let alone whether he had Arianna's keys or not. "I don't know. I'll have to check when I get home."

There was an awkward silence. They gazed at each other, then burst out laughing. "This is silly," Ben said, once he had his breath back. He rose from his chair behind the desk and came around to take Anna's hand. "I'm glad you came by," he told her, squeezing her hand gently.

Anna blushed. "Me, too." She coughed. "My keys are in the pocket of your jeans. I saw you put them there last night," she confessed. Once again they laughed.

"Why don't I finish up here, and then we can go over to the diner and grab a bite to eat?" Ben asked. Anna had no objections, and, after Ben cleared his desk, they stepped out into the bright sunshine. Conversation was lively, and after their meal they strolled hand in hand through town. People occasionally stopped to watch the young couple, smiling at the sight they made, Ben tall and handsome, Anna petite and beautiful.

They walked back to the church, then Ben gave Anna a lift to the hotel. He stopped to chat with Janice, but begged off staying since he was still working on tomorrow's sermon. Anna marveled that the past week had just flown by. She sauntered up to her room, unable to get the smile off her face. The time she had spent with Ben the last two days left her feeling excited about the future. For the first time, she didn't feel the urge to run to the next assignment to avoid a relationship.

"Too bad I have to go this time," she told herself as she prepared for bed that night. Lauren wanted *Whispering Wilds* finished in two weeks, and the white water rafting trip she was suppose to document was to take place the week after that.

Anna spent most of the next day on the phone making arrangements for the rafting trip, and with the State Park system, making sure she wouldn't need any special permits to work in the state park near Jordon. No special permit was needed, she was told, and they would send her a park pass in the mail. The man on the phone had a copy of her last book and was very excited that Anna planned to finish her new book with photos taken in 'his' state park.

When she emerged from her room in search of food, she found Ben sitting on the patio with Janice. They appeared to be deep in conversation, so Anna grabbed a soda and the sandwich Janice had left for her, before walking loudly through the room. At the sound of her steps both people turned to see who was approaching.

Ben's heart lightened when he saw Arianna walking toward him. He had been talking to Janice for almost an hour, telling her his worries about pursuing a relationship with Arianna. Janice quietly reminded him that not all men were not meant to live alone forever. Although he was still uncertain if Anna was 'the one', he couldn't deny that his feelings for her were strong. Now that she had finally come back to the Lord, he was comfortable dating her, although he still wasn't sure dating for him was a good idea. He hoped her feelings about it weren't as confusing as his were.

He rose from his seat as she approached, and pulled out a chair for her. "Thanks," she said, a bright smile on her face. It felt nice to be treated like a lady. He returned to his seat when she was settled.

"So where have you been hiding yourself?" he wanted to know. "I missed you in church this morning."

Anna blushed in embarrassment. "Sorry. Lauren called

very early this morning, to make sure I had made all the arrangements I needed to take care of. The white water rafting company needed confirmation by today."

"White water rafting?" Ben asked, surprised.

"Yeah. They're in the process of revamping their brochures and hired me to do it. I keep forgetting. Lauren's had to remind me several times."

Ben frowned. "It sounds kind of dangerous, doesn't it?"

Anna laughed. "No. It's not like it's the first time I've ever done it. I worked on one in Colorado a few summers ago."

There was silence for a moment while Ben thought about it. He wasn't used to such adventuresome women. This was definitely going to take some getting used to. But then again, he loved the outdoors. Arianna would be a wonderful sight to wake up to in the wild, came an unbidden thought. Where did that come from, Ben wondered silently. Aloud he said, "I guess it could be fun. I must admit, I've never gone."

They spent the next hour talking about some of the trips Anna had taken. Then she told him that she was also planning a trip to the state park near Jordon to finish up *Whispering Wilds*. "The man on the phone seemed pleased that the park was going to be in the book," Anna informed Ben and Janice.

"Are you really going to include our park?" Janice questioned with excitement.

"I sure am, Janice. I think it would be nice to include some eastern shots in this book. *Soaring Eagles* was almost exclusively west coast work."

"When are you planning on taking the pictures," Ben wanted to know.

Anna thought about that for a minute. "I'm not sure. With spring starting it's possible I could run into tourists if I went on the week-end. And I think I might need two trips."

"If you want, I can take you on one of those trips. There's a great place to watch flying squirrels that I know of," Ben offered.

"That sounds great, Ben. But what would people think of their pastor going off into the wild with an unmarried young lady?"

Ben grinned, then looked at Janice. "We can take Janice with us. She can be our chaperone."

Janice frowned at him. "I don't think so, young man. I can't see myself traipsing through the woods in a cast. I doubt anyone would put up a fuss about you two, but if you're really worried about it, Anna," the woman said turning to Anna, "then take a couple of the teens with you. They're enough of a chaperone for anyone."

The trio got a good laugh out of that. Although said in a joking manner, Anna was serious in her concern about Ben's reputation. She thought Janice's suggestion had merit and told Ben so. He promised to check with the youth on Tuesday, when he met with some at an evening Bible study.

"See if they can make it Thursday through Saturday," Anna asked. "As long as their parent's don't mind them missing two days of school," she added. "That way we'll be leaving the park when the weekenders are arriving."

He said he would, then casually asked her if she had any plans for the rest of the evening.

"Other than the evening service, no," Anna answered.

"Great," Ben grinned. "I thought we could go out for ice cream afterwards."

"If I'm not careful, you're going to have to roll me around. All this rich food," Anna joked.

Ben looked her over carefully. "Oh, I don't think that would be a problem." He liked the way Arianna looked. Not thin, not fat, and all that glorious hair. His gray eyes twinkled at her, making her blush.

Oh how I wish I could stop that, she moaned to herself. Ben must have read her mind, because the grin on his face grew larger, and he seemed to be having trouble containing a snicker. He excused himself shortly after that to get ready for church.

Anna, in light of her upcoming ice cream date with Ben, dressed casually in a pair of white chinos and yellow cotton sweater that highlighted her auburn hair and light tan.

The service that evening was short. It was kids night, so Ben surrendered his duties to a few of the teens from the youth group. The younger children made up the choir for the evening, and led the church in some of their favorite songs. Ben had a short meeting with the youth and their parents after the service. He decided that waiting until Tuesday to tell them about a possible camping trip would cause too much pressure. Most of the group decided against it, but there were three who were very interested. Since their parents had no objections to their missing school, it was decided that everyone would meet at Ben's bright and early Thursday morning and they would leave from there. They would discuss it in depth after the Bible study Tuesday night.

Ben passed along the news to Arianna as they walked hand in hand to the ice cream parlor. "We should have no problem with these three. They're the most devoted out of the group."

"Oh, I'm not worried," Anna assured him. "That's what you're along for. Crowd control!" They both laughed. "But, seriously, we will have to make sure they are extremely quiet while I'm working. Some of the shots I'm looking for could take quite a while."

Ben pushed open the door to the ice cream shop. "It will be interesting to watch you work," he told Arianna as they placed their order. "I'm really looking forward to it."

Anna glowed. She had been praised for her work by some famous people, but she had never felt as wonderful as she did when Ben praised her. She could feel the tell tale blush creeping into her cheeks, but decided to ignore it.

The two ate their ice cream as they walked to the town square. They sat on one of the benches and watched as people strolled by. Anna explained to Ben about the book she wanted to do about Jordon. He was excited by the idea, and felt it could do a lot for the town.

"It's slowly dieing," Ben said sadly. "The young men and women feel that there's no life here for them, so they go off to the big cities and don't come back. We need to find a way to keep them here, give them jobs to look forward to. Perhaps tourism is the answer."

"I don't know, Ben," Anna replied. "After living in Los Angeles for so long, I find it so peaceful here. I'd hate to see that go if crowds were to come."

"It doesn't have to be that way. If we promote the town as a quiet place to rest and relax, but with other attractions, like the lakes and mountains, we should be able to do all right." They debated the subject a while longer, then walked back to the church.

"I have a few things to do to get ready for the trip," Anna told Ben as he helped her into her Jeep. "I'll be out of town until Tuesday afternoon."

Ben looked startled. "Why so long?" he questioned.

Anna was amused. He sounded almost like Lauren. "It takes a lot of work to do one of my trips, Ben."

Now he looked nervous. "Exactly what are you planning on doing to me and my unsuspecting youth group," he demanded, with a twinkle in his eye.

"Oh I don't know," she twinkled back. "I'm sure I can think of something."

"Is there anything I can help with?" he asked, serious now.

Anna thanked him with a look."No, there really isn't, Ben. There are just certain things I have to do myself."She snapped her fingers in remembrance. "There is one thing. Think you could handle food for the trip? I'm usually only feeding myself. I'm not sure I'd get enough stuff for all five of us."

"Sure, no problem. I'm used to feeding a crowd."

"I have a camp stove, and I'll check with the park ranger about having fires."

"O.K. Be careful, wherever you're going," he said. He cupped her face in his hands, and gave her a gentle kiss on the lips. "Remember me."

As he turned and walked away, Anna's fingers reached up and touched her lips where he had kissed her. A soft smile lit her face as she put the Jeep in gear and drove off. "Remember him, he says," Anna said, grinning broadly. "How could I forget him? I think I'm in love with him."

Ten

Bright and early Monday morning, Anna headed her Jeep in the direction of Williamsburg. If she was taking three teens and Ben with her on her upcoming trip, she would have to get a few more camping supplies, and the store in Williamsburg had been a good one. She hummed along with the radio as she drove, happily thinking of the things she had to do. Although she always loved her photography trips, this one would be even more special because Ben would be there.

As she lay in bed the night before, she thought of some great things to do for the new book. Although this trip was to finish up *Whispering Wilds*, she would also be taking some pictures for the book about Jordon. Just before drifting off to sleep the idea had come to her. Why not let the teens take some of the pictures. They didn't have to be of animals. This book was to be about the whole town of Jordon, and weren't these teens part of the town? Getting pictures of each other would be fun for them, and also keep them occupied while Anna was doing her own work. It would probably lighten Ben's load as well.

Now as she drove, she made a mental list of the places she needed to visit in town. Of course, the camping store, but also a photography store. She wanted to pick up another inexpensive camera for the kids and Ben to use. Plus she was running out of film. She also needed to call Lauren to see if Lance had shown up yet.

Thinking of Lance brought a cloud to Anna's sunny horizon. Her feelings for Ben were strong. She was positive she was in love with him. Maybe Ben would let his feelings be known this weekend. But Lance was still out there, somewhere, thinking that he and Anna were a couple. She had to set things straight before anything permanent could happen between her and Ben.

Anna smiled at the thought of permanence. Wouldn't it be wonderful to wake up to that smile every morning, Anna thought dreamily.

The time seemed to fly by, and before she knew it, Anna was in Williamsburg. After settling in her hotel, she began her preparations. The people at the camping store remembered her, and were most helpful. Several hours later, she had everything she and her group would need. The photography store was equally helpful, especially when they found out who she was. Lugging her purchases back to her room, Anna collapsed on a chair to catch her breath.

When she was rested, Anna picked up the phone and punched in Lauren's work number. The woman was practically a workaholic, so Anna was fairly certain she would be in. She was rewarded when Lauren herself picked up.

"Hilltop Publishing," she said.

"I have a question about one of your authors," Anna said in the deepest voice she could muster.

"And I have all the answers," Lauren parried back. "How are you, Arianna?"

Anna laughed. "How did you know it was me?" she joked.

"You're the only person I know who has questions about my authors. So what's up?"

"A couple of things, actually. I head out into the wild on Thursday to finish up *Whispering Wilds*."

"Terrific!"

"I'm taking a few others with me," Anna informed her.

Lauren gave a disbelieving snort. "You? Miss "I prefer to work alone"? I wonder who it could be?"

"Don't get smart, Lauren," Anna told her. "I need to ask you something serious. Have you heard from Lance?"

Lauren turned serious, too. "No, Anna, no one has. Even the company that hired him for this movie is beginning to wonder. His agent said they don't begin shooting for another three weeks, but the director wanted to talk through a few scenes."

Anna shook her head. She wondered what Lance was up to. It wasn't like him to just blow off a movie. He was much to vain for that. "I need to talk to him."

"About anything special?"

"Hinting for information, Lauren," Anna teased. "You don't have to. I think, no, I'm sure. I'm in love with Ben."

Lauren screamed over the phone, and Anna held it away from her ear, smiling. "That's terrific. I'm so happy for you. Who is Ben and how does he feel?"

"Ben is a man I met here, and for how he feels, well, I don't know for sure, but I would like to say it's mutual. We've known each other for a few weeks. The last time Lance called here, Ben was the one who spoke to him. Lance told him a few, shall we say, intimate things about me. Ben was steamed. Later he told me it was jealousy that made him react that way. We've gone out a few times since then, and without going into details, it was wonderful."

"Oh, come on Arianna, please go into details," Lauren begged.

Anna laughed. "I'll never kiss and tell."

"You kissed? Was it wonderful?"

This time she couldn't hold back her sigh of pleasure. "It was beautiful," she whispered. She listened to Lauren teasing her for a few minutes longer, but then broke in. "I need to get going Lauren. But please call me if Lance gets back. If I'm not around leave a message with Janice at my hotel."

They hung up, and Anna sat quietly pondering, her mind moving from problems with Lance, to love with Ben. A smile lit her face as she drifted off into a doze. She woke up a short time later still smiling. After dinner, and a swim in the hotel pool she took herself off to bed, dreaming of a man with warm gray eyes.

The next morning, Anna finished her preparations for her trip to the state park. She made one last trip to the camping store, then packed her Jeep and headed back to Jordon. The trip was warm and pleasant, and Anna drove with the top off letting the wind whip through her hair. She felt carefree, and so happy, and knew that it was more than just her love for Ben that was making her feel that way.

Since renewing her commitment to Christ, Anna had felt such peace, peace like she had never known before. And she had Ben to thank for that. If she hadn't been attracted to him, she may had gone on as before, floating from place to place with no plan. Now she was letting Christ lead her, and she was thankful that the Lord seemed to be directing her to Ben.

Ben's place was on the way into town, so Anna decided to stop and say hello. If she were being honest with herself, she would have to admit it was because she missed him, but she decided that now was not the time to be honest. She laughed aloud. Even now she was kidding herself. She missed him so much she felt like throwing herself in his arms. That won't do, she admonished herself, as she jumped out of the driver's seat. He might run screaming for the hills.

Anna was still giggling when Ben came around the front of the house. She had her head up looking at the sky, so she didn't see him approach, but he had a wonderful view of her. Her copper colored hair flowed in waves down her back, shooting off red sparks in the sunshine. She was dressed in faded jeans and a white camp shirt, and she looked so good he wanted to grab hold of her and never let her go.

Ben couldn't control the urge to hold her close. Before she even knew he was there, she was wrapped in his arms. Startled at first, Anna's eyes flew to meet his. When she realized who it was, she relaxed into the embrace, leaning against his chest. It felt so right. Her arms coiled around his neck, and she rested her head against his shoulder.

"I've missed you," she whispered. A contented sigh was all she heard in response, but it was enough. They stood that way for some time before Ben pulled back. When Anna looked up, his gray eyes were smiling, but there was something else there that made her catch her breath. She couldn't put words to the look, but it spoke to her heart in a way that words couldn't. He bent his head and lightly brushed her lips with his.

Looking down into Arianna's eyes, Ben lost himself in the feelings shown there. He was in love with this woman, and if the glow in those chocolate brown eyes were any indication, Arianna felt the same way. Ben wasn't sure what the future held for them, but he felt certain that there could be a future for them. He had prayed unceasingly over the last two days, desiring to know God's will for his life. When Arianna had appeared moments ago, he had been in prayer about them, specifically asking the Lord if he should pursue the relationship. Ben gave another contented sigh. Thank you, Lord, he breathed silently, for answered prayer.

"I'm happy you're home," he told her, hugging her tightly then letting her go. They walked hand in hand to the house, where Ben sat her on the sofa. He went into the kitchen and came back with two glasses of ice tea, and some chips.

"Not as glad as I am to be here," Anna replied, taking a sip of her tea. "I finished all my last minute details," she informed him. "What about you?"

He gave her a look that could melt butter. "Oh, I managed O.K." He didn't speak again until he had drained his glass. "The kids are very excited. I'm not sure it will even be worth having Bible study tonight," he teased. "I have a feeling all they're going to be talking about is this trip."

Anna laughed. "That might not be a bad idea, come to think of it. I'd like to go over some ground rules with the kids, and this might not be a bad time. If it's all right with you, of course."

Ben contemplated Anna's wish for a moment before answering. "I think that would be fine, but what about the other kids?"

"I'm sorry, Ben. I didn't even think about that."

He stood and faced the fireplace, obviously thinking about something. "Maybe this might work better. I'll have our study, same as usual, but cut it short. It normally ends at eight thirty. If I end at seven forty-five, that gives you forty-five minutes to go over the camping trip with the three that are going. I can get the others home if they need a ride, and be back in time to take you out for a late dinner."

"Late dinner," she looked at him innocently. "I don't remember mentioning a late dinner."

"There are some things I can think of on my own, thank you very much." He glanced over at the clock. "Oops, I've got to get moving." He picked up their empty glasses, setting them in the sink, and coming back out to her. "I have a meeting with one of the men from the board in twenty minutes."

Anna jumped up. "I"m sorry, Ben. I didn't realize you were in a hurry to get somewhere. Why didn't you say something?"

As Arianna moved toward the door, Ben grabbed her around the waist and pulled her to him. "I don't remember complaining. I'm very glad you came by." He turned her to face him and gave her a lengthy kiss. "Very glad."

This time Anna sighed with contentment. Ben laughed and then walked her to the Jeep. "Be at the church at seven thirty, Arianna," he said as he shut her door. She smiled her agreement, and Ben watched as she drove away.

As he drove toward town, his thoughts turned to his upcoming meeting. It was at Ben's urging that this meeting was taking place. He wanted to bounce a few ideas off the church's board chairman before he made any final decisions. Ben was confident Richard Weston would give him sound advice.

"Thanks for coming, Richard," Ben said as he shook the man's hand. They were seated in Ben's office, the door closed securely against any unwanted interruptions. "I know you're busy, but it's important."

For the next hour, the two men discussed and debated various issues Ben brought up. When it was over, both men were satisfied that God's will was being done. They parted, Richard for his home, to pray, and Ben to his office to get ready for the evening's Bible study, which was set to begin in less than an hour.

The kids were hyper, as Ben had figured they would be, but he managed to get them under control. The study that evening was based on Proverbs. The group was concentrating on how they should act, and Ben thought the Proverbs were a good place to start. Everything written there about fools was a real eye-opener to some, who guiltily lowered their eyes when some of the passages were read.

"We aren't here to pass judgment on anyone," Ben was quick to assure the teens. "We are here to learn to be God's people. My grandfather had me read a Proverb a day, every day. It really sunk in. So that's my challenge to you," Ben said as they closed. "Read a Proverb everyday as well as your regular reading. We'll meet next Tuesday to see how it's going."

Ben turned when he heard Arianna stirring behind him. "Now, for those of you involved in the camping trip, Miss Jenkins has a few things to go over with you. Anyone need a ride?" he asked those who were rising to leave. Two teens raised their hands, so Ben gathered them together. "Just a second," he waved to them. "Arianna," he whispered, lowering himself to where she sat. "I'll have to take a raincheck on dinner tonight." She looked up at him startled. "I have to make a phone call, and it could take awhile."

Anna was disappointed. She had been looking forward to being alone with him, but the look on his face told her he was very preoccupied. "That's all right, Ben."

Ben silently conveid thanks to Anna for not asking questions. Looking down into her sweet face, he was having the hardest time not kissing her. "How about breakfast? I can pick you up about seven."

"Seven? You mean, I like have to wake up early?" she moaned, trying to hide the gleam in her eyes.

At first he was wounded by her rejection, but then he caught the light in her dark brown eyes. "I could make it six."

"Oh no, seven is fine," she laughed.

That settled, Ben left with his two students, and Anna faced the three who were to accompany her and Ben on the camping trip. She handed each of them a list of instructions. "I know you all have probably done this before," she said, smiling. "But not with me. Because of the work I need to do on this trip, things might be a little different." For the next half hour they went over some of her rules, and also some of the things they should bring.

"I have a surprise for you, too." Anna had their attention with the word surprise. "I've started work on another book and I would like the three of you to help me." The students looked stunned. "Don't all talk at once," she joked.

She explained what she wanted them to do, which they had no problem with. She closed the meeting with prayer, then told them to meet at Ben's by five thirty Thursday morning. Anna went home satisfied that it was going to be a trip to remember.

Eleven

It was still dark when Anna pulled into Ben's driveway Thursday morning at five o'clock. She had informed Ben at breakfast the day before that she would be there a half hour before the kids in order to get everything together. Ben had groaned, but she sweetly reminded him that she had gotten up early for him, it was only fair he did so for her. She only grinned when he complained that five was a lot earlier than seven.

He greeted her at the door with a large mug of chocolate flavored coffee. When her eyebrows rose in surprise, he gave a sly smile. "I have my ways," he said, pulling at an imaginary mustache. Anna laughed and accepted the mug, taking a long drink from it.

Ben led her to the sofa, drawing her down next to him. He took the mug out of her hands and set it on the table. "I'm glad you suggested us meeting first," he told her. "I've been dying to do this for days." He wrapped his arms around her, giving her a lingering kiss.

Anna melted into the kiss with a soft sigh. She wanted this herself. When Ben finally lifted his head, she laid her hand against his cheek. "That was wonderful," she whispered. As he bent his head again, Anna reluctantly drew back. "As much as I would like to continue this, we really should be getting our camping stuff together."

Ben was loath to let her go, but knew she was right. "All right," he sighed, "but I want us to take up where we left off when we get back." He jumped up from the sofa and hauled Anna up after him. He snatched a quick peck, then pulled her into the kitchen to show her the food stuffs he had for the trip.

"You must really know what you're doing," Anna admired. Ben had everything neatly packaged in manageable weights, so everyone could share in the chore of carrying the food.

Ben blew on his fingertips then rubbed them against his chest. "Oh, I've camped a bit," he remarked smugly. "I'm not sure if the kids have backpacks, though. I forgot to ask."

"Well, I didn't. They do, thank heaven. I'd hate for them to have to hike with a pack that doesn't fit. It's so uncomfortable."

The two of them carried the packs of food out to Ben's truck, after deciding to load up the backpacks once they reached the base camp. The teens arrived a short time later, and there was general pandemonium as good-byes were said, and last minute commands given by the parents. Then they were on their way, Anna's Jeep loaded with the kids and Ben's truck laden with the luggage.

The trip to the park entrance was filled with chattering voices, each one determined to be the loudest. Anna just smiled. It had been a long time since she had been in the company of such enthusiastic companions, and she was enjoying every minute of it.

The guard at the gate gave Anna directions to the base camp where they were to park. They followed the road through dense trees and high grass until finally pulling into a gravel parking lot. "We're here," she called, jumping out of the Jeep. Ben rounded the front of his truck, meeting her within seconds.

He stood, looking up the mountain, clearly visible in the light of dawn. "Quite a trek you have planned for us, Ms. Jenkins," he commented.

"Oh, I'm sure you can handle it Reverend Thompson," she replied. The students were roaming the lot, when Anna called them to order. Shortly thereafter, backpacks were loaded, and they were off, Anna in the lead and Ben bringing up the rear.

As they hiked along, Ben was able to admire the way Arianna moved. She had a lithe grace about her despite her small stature. Her copper hair was pulled into a high pony tail that swung from side to side as she strode along. Although sunglasses hid them from view, Ben knew those brown eyes were glowing with happiness. Her whole demeanor was one of total and complete contentment.

Her camera was around her neck, and Anna was constantly snapping pictures, both of the scenery and of the group as they hiked through the rough terrain. The kids were eating it up, acting as hammy as they possibly could. More than once Ben heard Arianna's laughter filling the air, and realized that he had never really heard her laugh before. He liked it, almost as much as he loved her.

"This is not going to be an easy week-end," he muttered to himself. Arianna was stirring feelings within him that he had never been tempted by before, and controlling those urges was going to be one of the hardest things he had ever done. Now I know what the kids feel like when those hormones are raging, he thought.

A scream from the one teenage girl on the trip brought Ben out of his musings. He looked up to see Marty Case dangling a fake spider in front of Joanne Harris, who was not taking the joke in the best way. Ben moved up to reprimand the boy, but before he could get there, Anna already had things in hand. Marty's fake spider was no match for Anna, who was retaliating with her own brand of humor. From the side of her pack, she had pulled out a can of silly string, and let it fly all over Marty, who ran screaming away from it. Unable to control herself, Anna dropped to her knees laughing so hard she couldn't catch her breath.

"Oh, I love that," she got out between gurgles of laughter. Joanne had joined her, as had the other boy, John White. Marty took the ribbing in good humor, dropping down next to his friends.

Ben walked up to the four of them shaking his head. "What am I going to do with you kids?" he tisked, shrugging off his pack and sitting down on a fallen log. Anna and the kids looked at him, then at each other, then burst out laughing again. It was several minutes before they had themselves in control once more.

Sitting in a rough circle, each pulled out their canteens and took a quick swig of their water. Anna informed them there was probably another two hours to hike before they reached the site where Anna wanted to set up camp. A collective groan went up from the kids and Ben. Anna just smiled.

When they were back on the track, Anna set a rather punishing pace, wanting to get to the camp before the noon sun made walking even more uncomfortable. She would let them rest while she set up camp. She kept a close eye on the three kids behind her, as did Ben. Anna could tell that he knew what her plan was, and he seemed to be in agreement. Up in the higher elevations the sun always seemed much harsher.

"We're here!" Anna announced finally, shedding her pack, and quickly helping the others to do the same. The kids instantly dropped to the ground, exhausted. "Sorry about the pace guys, but you'll be thanking me pretty soon. The sun will be at its highest point shortly, and it's going to get hot." She went around offering water to each of them, Ben included, who was now resting against a large boulder on the edge of the clearing.

Ben looked at Arianna in admiration. She wasn't even winded. As good of shape as he thought he was in, this had still been a hard trip for him. It had been ages since he had made such an extensive hike, and he was feeling it. But Anna was going around the camp as if she did this everyday.

When she started putting up the tents, Ben felt obligated to drag himself to his feet and help her. She giggled when she saw him walking towards her. He looked wiped out. "You don't have to help, Ben, I can manage," she told him, a gentle smile on her face.

Ben returned the smile. "I can't let you do this by yourself. It wouldn't be fair."

She stayed his arm as he reached for a tent post. "Don't, Ben." He looked at her in confusion. "I didn't invite you here to do work. I can really take care of this myself. All you need to do is keep track of the kids, and make sure they keep out of trouble. And relax."

"What do you mean, relax?" Ben questioned

Anna looked him full in the face. "You've been very distracted lately," she commented.

He leered at her. "I've had reason to be."

Crimson spread over Anna's face. "I don't mean because of me!" she hissed softly. The kids were watching them curiously.

Ben grinned unrepentantly. "I don't know," he drawled. "You may not mean to be, but you sure are mighty diverting."

"Ben!" She looked him squarely in the eyes. "I'm serious."

"O.K." he relented. "I know I've had a few things on my mind lately. But I promise that I'll get plenty of rest and relaxation on this trip."

Despite her protests, they worked together to put up the tents, in a large triangle around a fire pit Anna made. She and Joanne would share one tent, Ben would take one, and the boys would share the other tent. Anna glanced around the area at the kids. She remembered her first climb, and how tired she had been that first day. The altitude had really gotten to her, but she had felt much better after a short nap.

"O.K. guys," she announced, standing in the center area. "I know you probably won't like this, but it's nap time." The teens groaned, protesting that they weren't little kids. "You'll feel like new people when you wake up. No complaining. This evening we'll take a short hike the park ranger recommended." Anna could tell they weren't happy about it, but they obeyed her anyway.

"You too, Ben," Anna added. She noticed that, although he was in excellent health, he seemed to be rather pooped out.

Ben frowned at her. "I don't want you out here alone, Arianna."

She just laughed. "Ben, I've been doing this alone for a

long time. I'll be fine. In fact it will be a perfect time to set up some shots. Don't make me use force," she teased.

"All right, I'll go," he capitulated. "But only if you promise not to go too far from camp." For some reason he didn't understand he was worried about Anna being alone.

"My first shots will be fairly close to camp," Anna assured him. With that Ben appeared satisfied and turned toward his tent.

Anna sat for several minutes on a log just outside the tents, thinking. Ben's request had surprised her, mostly because she wasn't used to anyone caring about where she was or what she did. In fact, until she had come to Jordon, the only person who had truly cared had been her mother. Even Lance only showed an interest if it would benefit him in some way. Silently praying, Anna thanked the Lord for the people now in her life.

When she was finished, Anna hefted her camera equipment onto her back and headed into the woods. It took several tries, but she finally found the perfect place to set up her camera. A rocky ledge overlooking a gorge gave her a wonderful perspective. From her vantage point she could see several areas where she was sure animals would be roaming. The ledge wasn't easily assessable, but Anna made sure she would be able to manage it even in the dark.

After she had everything set to her satisfaction, Anna glanced at her watch and was shocked to see that two hours had passed. Unless she missed her guess, Ben would be sending out search parties soon. She hurriedly packed up what she was taking back with her, and rushed back to camp.

Anna wasn't far from the mark. When she returned to the camp, Ben was prowling around like a caged bear. "Where have you been?" he demanded. Noticing the kids listening, he lowered his voice, and lightened his tone.

Resting a hand on his arm, she soothed, "I lost track of time, Ben. But I was fine."

Ben looked down at her hand laying on his arm. He still hadn't figured out why he was so worried, and had been in prayer about it, but with each minute that passed Anna's absence weighed heavily on his heart. "I'm sorry, Arianna. I really don't know what the matter is."

His voice sounded so down, Anna was quick to reassure him. "I promise not to do anything foolish, Ben. I'm grateful that someone actually cares enough to worry."

As much as he wanted to, Ben knew he couldn't pull her into his arms and kiss her. To prevent himself from doing just that, he linked his arms behind his back. But his eyes told her how much it was costing him. "I care enough to worry," he said instead.

Anna smiled, completely understanding his dilemma. The tension eased between them, and they turned to the kids. "I found a place for my camera," she informed everyone. "Now, you have to promise that you will be quiet when I ask you to be. I'm usually alone, so this is a new experience for me."

"Miss Jenkins?" Joanne asked.

"Yes?"

"You said at the meeting that you wanted us to help with your new book. What are we going to be doing?"

Anna smiled. "Just being yourselves. All four of you," she said, including Ben in her statement, "will have time with this new camera I have. I want pictures of the scenery, of course, but I also want pictures of you all having fun."

The kids thought that was cool. Ben kept his thoughts to himself. He'd have to limit his time with the camera or else there would only be pictures of Anna on the roll. He was still daydreaming when Anna's voice cut through his thoughts.

"...tomorrow night."

Ben looked up, knowing he was going to have to find out what was going on. "Uh, tomorrow night, what?" he asked. His face heated up at the exasperated look she gave him.

"Tomorrow night I'll take you all out to another site, and you can watch some of the night life around here."

"Oh."

She let the kids go, reminding them to stay within sight of the camp, then turned to Ben. "Are you sure you're all right?"

"Well, that depends."

"On what?"

"On if I can manage to keep my hands off you, and my lips to myself."

Anna was startled for a minute, then grinned. "I'm sure a tough guy like you can handle that," she told him.

He groaned. "I hope you know that this is the hardest thing I've ever had to do."He turned serious. "I mean it, Arianna. It's going to be hard not touching you. But I'm the pastor of the church, and what kind of example would I be if I can't manage to control myself."

She returned his look. "Ben, you need to relax. I know exactly what you mean. It's not exactly easy for me either. But you can do this."She grinned. "By tomorrow, after not showering for a while, you won't have any problems staying away from me."

Ben laughed. Anna always seemed to know how to reach him, even when he couldn't seem to get a grip on his thoughts. And she had a great sense of humor. "You're right," he admitted. "But Arianna," he warned, "we have to talk when this trip is over."

She wasn't sure what he meant, and before she could ask, the teens returned from their explorations, remarking on how hungry they were. Ben and John got the fire ready, then Ben started preparing the meal.

Sitting back, replete, Anna sighed. "I could get used to this," she told Ben, handing him her plate. "I have to do my own cooking when I'm in the field. I usually just buy the stuff where you just add water."

Ben looked aghast. "Just add water! No way! Gramps taught me how to do a meal right."

"Thank heaven for Gramps," she grinned. The teens agreed.

By the time clean-up was finished it was growing late.

The sun was lowering in the sky, and Anna decided it was time for her to get to work. "I'm going to head out now, Ben," she told him, gathering some snacks to slip into her backpack.

"Are you sure you'll be all right?" He still couldn't shake his feeling that something was going to happen to her.

She reached out to brush her fingers across his cheek."I'm positive, Ben." She pulled a sheet of paper out of her pocket. "This is a rough map to where I'll be." Ben took the proffered paper and looked at it, turning it this way and that. Then he looked at Arianna. "O.K. So it's a very rough map. I'm set up about a mile away." She moved over to her tent, went in, then came out with a walkie-talkie in her hand. She gave it to Ben. "I used these with Terri, on the last trip I took. It seemed to work well. If either of us were in trouble, we called."

Ben felt much better, knowing he could contact her. "Just leave it on, all right?"

"I promise," she whispered. "I'm going to be late, so try not to stay up," she said, knowing he would be waiting for her when she got back.

Ben knew she knew, and smiled guiltily. He gave her hand a squeeze, then Anna was hiking out of camp. He set the kids a few more clean-up tasks then had a short Bible study. When they were finished he sent them to their tents. He sat down in front of the fire, spending the time reading his Bible and praying. Praying for the changes in his life he knew were coming, and praying for Anna, whose safety was weighing so heavily on his mind.

Anna made the mile trek to her camera site in record time. There was still enough light for her to find a comfortable position, and pull things out of her pack in readiness for the night ahead. Too much movement would scare the animals away, so she placed anything she thought she might need within easy reach. One camera was set on a tripod, able to swing easily in any direction, the other hung around her neck.

She grabbed her binoculars and did a quick survey. Nocturnal animals were starting to make their appearance. Owls flying above, their voices calling out, the scurrying of little feet dodging in and out of foliage. The sounds of the night were a soothing balm to Anna's fraying nerves.

Even though she had made light of it, Anna took Ben's fear of her safety very seriously. She herself had felt pricklings of anxiety all the way up the mountain. She had put it down to worry about the kids, if something were to happen to one of them, but Ben seemed so positive that Anna herself was in danger. She didn't quite know what to make of it, but decided the best course of action would be to give it over to the Lord in prayer.

The peace Anna received from praying lasted the whole evening. She put her troubled heart to rest, at least for the time being, and, concentrating on her work, was rewarded with some fantastic shots. She was quite pleased with her night's labor as she stuffed paraphernalia into her backpack. She hoisted it onto her back, and was walking towards camp when she felt the first niggling of fear. Something wasn't quite right. She felt like she was being watched, but that was ridiculous. Other than those with her, there was no one around for miles. The park ranger had informed her that no other hiking party was in the area.

Anna hurried along the path, alert to everything around her. There was still a half mile to go when a shadow crossed her path about a hundred feet in front of her. Anna stopped and stood motionless. In front of her a very large black bear paused in the path. The ranger had mentioned them, but was fairly sure there weren't any in the area. Well, so much for that, Anna thought to herself. The bear stopped for a moment, staring at her. Then losing interest, he meandered on his way.

Heaving a trembling sigh, Anna also continued, keeping a wary eye out for the roving bear. When she stepped into camp, there was Ben, laying on top of his sleeping bag, next to the fire. He appeared to be sleeping, but when Anna approached him, he rolled over to look into her eyes.

"You're frightened," he stated.

Anna sat down next to him. "Yes, I was," she admitted.

"There was a bear about a half mile out of camp. He gave me a look, but must have had better prospects."

Ben sat up, taking Anna in his arms. She let him hold her for a minute, then pulled away. "I'm all right," she insisted. "And I don't think he'll bother us. But we should hang the food just in case."

He nodded his agreement, and they set to work. It was very late when they finished. Ben watched her as they worked. She seemed calm, but she had been trembling in his arms before. "Are you sure you're all right?" he questioned, looking directly into her big brown eyes.

"Yes." She held his gaze, knowing in her heart that even though she had been frightened on the trail, standing here with Ben she felt perfectly safe.

"Then I'll see you in the morning," he whispered, gently brushing her lips with his. He led her to her tent, then made his way to his own. When he looked back over his shoulder, Anna was watching him. She gave him a wave, then entered her tent.

Morning came too soon. Anna had had a hard time falling asleep last night, her mind wandering from her feelings for Ben to the bear and back again. It was the early hours before she drifted off, and she wasn't ready to face the morning just yet. The teens, on the other hand, were revved and ready to go after their early night the evening before. Ben had tried to keep them quiet so Anna could lie in, but trying to keep them quiet was like trying to muffle an exploding atom bomb.

She rose reluctantly, and smiled in appreciation when Ben met her at her tent door with a steaming cup of coffee. "I thought you might be able to use a pick me up," he told her when they were seated around the fire ring. "I'll have your breakfast ready shortly."

Anna stretched. "You know? I'll have to think about this traveling alone bit. It's nice to wake up to someone else doing the cooking."

Ben took a quick look around before answering. "I'd be

happy to cook for you," he offered, his eyes saying he'd do a lot more.

When she had finished her breakfast, Anna led the kids around the area pointing out various plants and animal tracks. They were lucky enough to see a few animals in action but most stayed away from the noisy teens. Anna gave the kid's camera to Marty for a bit, and he instantly began snapping away. She smiled at his enthusiasm, and at how hammy the other two were becoming. John hung upside down from a low hanging branch of a huge oak tree, and Joanne posed behind him holding a large stick, as if using it for a bat and John for a ball.

As evening came, the group sat around the campfire while Ben threw together a filling and delicious dinner. Not the ritz, he thought to himself as he dished out the steaming stew, but rather good if I have to say so myself. Which I probably will, he grinned, watching the two young boys fall on their food as if starving. Joanne ate at a much slower and more ladylike pace, and had the grace to thank Ben for making such a great dinner. The boys, realizing their lack of manners, promptly offered their thanks as well.

Ben turned to Anna, waiting for her appreciation, but, instead, found her staring off in another direction, totally ignoring what was going on around her. That she was preoccupied with something was obvious to Ben, but what he didn't know. When the teens finished and she was still holding her full bowl of stew, Ben grew worried. He stood, and casually meandered over to where she was sitting, leaning up against a fallen tree.

"Penny for your thoughts," he said softly, sitting beside her. Anna turned her head to face him, but didn't answer. Her dark brown eyes were troubled, he noted. "What's the problem, Arianna?"

She looked away for a moment. Her thoughts were in a jumble. To match my life, she silently grimaced. "I just don't know, Ben. I feel so mixed up inside. There's so much happening and I don't know how to handle it."

"I didn't realize so much was going on," he replied, taking the bowl from her hands, and grasping them within his own. "I know you're struggling with your emotions, Arianna." She made to deny it, but he squeezed her hand and shook his head to silence her. "I know, because I'm going through the same things myself. This trip may not have been the best idea. But I for one intend to make the most of it."

Ben bent his head and gently kissed her lips. "For now, let's just work on getting your book done. Maybe with that pressure off, we can start again, to get to know each other."

Anna looked up at his face, shadowed in the evening light. "It's not you, Ben," she told him softly. "At least not really. It's other problems, the ones I've been avoiding for the last few months. When I finally let Christ back into my life, I realized there would be some house cleaning to do. I'm just overwhelmed by how much of it there is."

"You don't have to do it alone, Arianna. That's the most wonderful part. His spirit is inside you, waiting to help." His finger ran gently down her cheek to rest on her lips. "I'm here to help, too."

"Thanks, Ben," Anna whispered. She leaned her head against his shoulder, and he wrapped her tightly in his embrace. They sat that way for several minutes, then Anna reluctantly pulled away. "I have to get going." When Ben made to protest, she hushed him by putting her hand over his mouth. "One more night and I'll be done."

Although he wanted to protest, he didn't. Instead, he helped her gather the things she needed, giving her a warm hug before she trudged out of camp. He watched her walking, her gait not the carefree one she had yesterday. One more night, he thought, a frown forming on his brow."Then what?" he muttered. Without an answer, he turned back to the camp, and the Bible study he had planned with the teens.

Twelve

Anna, wandering down the path to her camera perch, wondered at her melancholy. This wasn't at all like her. Normally her time spent in the mountains was filled with contentment. Then it hit her. Tonight was their last night. Saturday afternoon Anna, Ben, and the teens would hike back down the mountain, and reality would return. And Anna's reality was that she had to settle her problem with Lance as soon as possible. If not, she knew her relationship with Ben couldn't go forward.

The night sounds soothed her troubled spirit. Those, combined with her prayers, helped her accomplish a profitable night's work despite her uneasy beginning. It was extremely late when she returned to camp, this time without any encounters with the black bear, but Ben was still seated at the fire, a cup of coffee in his hand. He rose, filled a cup for her, then guided her to a place next to him.

They sat in companionable silence, Anna's head leaning on Ben's shoulder. "I could get used to this," he whispered, turning his head to kiss the top of her head. He tightened his hold on her momentarily. "I don't want to rush you, Arianna. I don't want to frighten you away from me."

She moved in his arms, until she was able to look up into his face. "You don't frighten me, Ben," she assured him. She laughed softly. "Although the way you look in the morning could possibly be considered scary."

He growled, and chucked her gently on the chin. "You aren't exactly Miss America, yourself," he bantered. "There are some things I need to sort out in my life, too, Anna," he continued, making a vague reference to the fact that Anna had things to sort out as well. "During the next few weeks, I'll be in and out of town, making some major decisions in my life." When

Anna looked at him in confusion, he did his best to reassure her. "I just wanted you to know. The time I've spent with you has been important to me, and I hope to you, too. But there are a few things that need to be done, and I may not be able to see much of you in the near future."

Anna lifted her head to better see Ben. His eyes were a somber gray, telling her he was truly unhappy about not seeing her. She brushed her finger down his cheek. "I can live with that, Ben. I have to finish my work, and next Thursday I'll be leaving on a four day rafting trip. After that, who knows. But I want you to know that you're very special to me, and I'll miss not being with you."

Ben wanted to kiss her so much his heart ached with it. But he knew that it would be much too hard to stop once he started, so instead, he took her hand and brought it up to his lips, where he feathered a kiss across her palm. Anna shivered, and it was almost Ben's undoing. He abruptly stood, almost toppling Anna in the process. Her indignant look eased his tension and made him grin.

"Sorry," he apologized, helping her up. "But if I don't go to bed now, who knows what will happen." He stuffed his hands in his pockets.

Anna felt frustrated, yet knew it was for the best. Although she had never had trouble keeping herself in check before, being in Ben's company was a whole different story. "I forgive you." She looked up at him. "Just don't let it happen again."

Her serious voice almost fooled him, but the twinkle in her eye gave her away. She was having just as hard a time as he was. It's good to know I'm not the only one having a problem, he told himself, as he shrugged into his sleeping bag a few moments later. He prayed for control before he drifted off to sleep.

The next morning came much to early for Ben and Anna. Anna struggled out of the daze of sleep, knowing she needed to get a couple of shots in the early morning hours before she was finished with the photography for *Whispering Wilds*. With that in mind she dragged on a pair of jeans and a sweatshirt, and stumbled out of the tent before Joanne was awake. In fact, there was no one awake yet. No coffee, Anna mourned silently, grabbing her camera. She scribbled a note for Ben, then headed out to the woods.

Ben heard someone stirring in camp, and hurried to get dressed, knowing Arianna would need a strong cup of coffee to get her going this morning. He stumbled out of the tent to see Marty and John fumbling with the cooking utensils.

"Hang on guys, I'm coming," Ben told them. He quickly began breakfast, having the boys help him. Joanne joined them, making the preparations go even faster.

"Where's Miss Jenkins?" Joanne asked as they sat around the fire with their plates.

Ben's head shot up. "What do you mean? I thought she was still sleeping."

Joanne looked over at him curiously. "No. She's not there."

Doing his best not to appear concerned, Ben finished his food, then cleared the mess from breakfast. His thoughts were in a whirl. Anna had gone to bed very late, and by her own admission, was not generally an early riser unless she had enough sleep. He bent over to return some cutlery to the food pack when he noticed a slip of paper. Cautiously, almost as if it would bite him, Ben opened the note. *Ben,* he read, *I wanted to get a few early morning shots. Don't be worried. I shouldn't be long. Arianna.*

He sighed in relief. He was still uncomfortable with Arianna's safety. Why it was bothering him so much he had no idea, but at least her absence this morning was work related. He left the campfire burning, knowing she would be dying for a cup of coffee on her return. Ben smiled.

Anna was indeed 'dying' for a cup of coffee. She could barely keep her eyes open. This late night stuff has to stop, she mumbled to herself. Luckily, she had been able to get the pictures she wanted without too much trouble. Usually, on days like these, it seemed like everything went wrong. She packed her equipment for the last time, and staggered back to camp.

When she entered the camp all was quiet, with no people in sight. Anna immediately headed for the coffee pot, sitting in the center of the campfire, thanking Ben profusely for thinking of her needs. She sat back against one of the logs, and breathed in the aroma of fresh coffee and wild flowers. After taking a long sip, her eyes closed, and soon she was sound asleep.

That's how Ben found her a half hour later when he and the teens returned to camp. He motioned the kids to stay quiet, and went over to remove the coffee cup held precariously in her hand. She didn't stir, and Ben decided she had best be moved to a more comfortable place. He lifted her gently in his arms, and carried her to his tent, which was situated the farthest from the center of camp. After settling her in his sleeping bag, he stared down at her. Tears stung his eyes at the feelings the sight of her evoked in him.

Several hours later, Anna awoke, stretching like a cat, trying to work the kinks out of her body. When she opened her eyes, she saw Ben sitting next to her, staring down with a soft smile on his face. "Hi, sleepy."

"Sorry," she apologized, sitting up. She then noticed she wasn't in her own tent. "Where am I?"

"I put you in my tent to give you some quiet. What time did you get up?" he wanted to know.

Anna brushed her fingers through her hair. "About five-thirty. I needed some sunrise shots, and realized last night that the spot I was using would be perfect for them. What time is it?"

Ben hid a grin. "Oh, about one o'clock."

Anna yelped. "What! Why did you let me sleep so late?" she demanded, pushing the sleeping bag aside. She grimaced at the sight she made. "We've got to get packed up."

"Already done, boss," he told her, helping her untangle herself. "You shouldn't have gone out when you were so tired, Arianna,"Ben reprimanded gently. "You could have gotten hurt."

"I know, but I really wanted the worked finished."

"Still, that's no reason to put yourself in danger. Don't do it again."

Anna looked at him questioningly. It wasn't like Ben to order people around, at least not in that tone of voice. "Is there something wrong, Ben?"

He had the grace to look sheepish. "No. I just can't seem to shake this feeling that you're in danger. It scares me."

She took his face in her hands. "Thank you for caring." She brushed her lips over his, then moved out of the tent. Ben sat there, feeling stunned. It was a good thing they were leaving today. He wasn't sure if he could control the roller coaster of emotions he was feeling for Arianna.

The group gathered together the rest of their things, rolled up the tents, and had one last devotion together before hiking down the mountain. John took his turn with the camera and chronicled the trip down, with the other two teens more than happy to clown around. Ben and Arianna also got into the act, much to the surprise of the youngsters.

"What? Do you think we're old fogeys or something?" Ben demanded to know, as he swung like a monkey from a low hanging branch.

Joanne didn't know what to say, but Marty and John had no such qualms. "Or something," they laughed at their pastor, knowing without a doubt that Ben was one of the coolest guys they knew. Ben grinned, and did a three sixty turn on the branch.

Anna watched with amusement. He is so good with kids, she thought. They gathered around him trying to help him from his perch. They were more of a hindrance, and before he knew it, Ben was sprawled face first on the ground. Anna burst out laughing, unable to control herself. He looked over at her, glowering.

"What are you laughing at?"

She grinned, swinging her camera around by it's strap. "Oh, nothing."

"Please tell me you don't have that on film."

"Well, I could tell you that, but then I would be lying."

He stood, and began moving in her direction. Anna scooted back, then turned to run, hearing Ben charging behind her. "I'll get you for that," his words followed her. Anna began giggling so much she couldn't run any more, and Ben caught her easily, wrapping his arms around her slim waist. "Gotcha!" His lips caressed her neck, sending shivers down her spine.

"Ben!" she protested in a whisper.

He stopped his nuzzling, but left his arms around her. "Sorry. Couldn't help myself." The teens coming up from behind forestalled any more conversation between them, but Ben gave up the pretense of keeping his distance from her. On the rest of the way down, he held her hand as much as possible. Anna had no objections. The teens gave them knowing snickers.

When the small company finally reached the vehicles, they were tired and dirty, but very happy. They quickly packed everything into the truck and headed back to Jordon. Instead of having their parents drive out to Ben's house, each teen was dropped, along with his dirty laundry, at their own home. With that taken care of Ben and Arianna each drove to McCray house.

"I can't stay," Ben told her as they moved equipment from the truck to the Jeep. When Anna looked at him questioningly he went on. "I have to prepare tomorrow's sermon yet, and there are a couple of meetings I need to set up. I hope you don't mind me leaving you all the clean-up to do."

Anna faced him, making her lips smile even though she didn't feel like it. She had been looking forward to spending some time alone with Ben this evening. "I don't mind. I need to inventory it anyway, to get ready for Thursday."

At the mention of her upcoming trip both of them became silent. Ben, because he knew it was unlikely he would be able to make time before Thursday to see her, and Anna because she was already missing Ben.

"Arianna," Ben said quietly. "I know this probably isn't going to come out right, but I'm going to be really busy for the next week or so. I don't think I'll be able to do much, other than work, for awhile. I'm sorry."

She looked at him sharply. He seemed regretful, yet Anna got the feeling he meant for more than 'just awhile'. "I don't know if I understand, Ben. Are you telling me you won't be able to see me for a day or two, or ever again?"

Ben squirmed uncomfortably. "I don't know if I'd say that. I just have a lot to do."

Confused, Anna mumbled a response. Ben's behavior at this moment was a complete turn around from just a few hours ago, when he said he was having trouble keeping his lips to himself. Her response must have been the end of the conversation as far as Ben was concerned, because he gave her a small smile, then got in his truck and drove away. When he was out of sight, Anna let out a tiny whimper. In one swift fell, her dreams of a future with Ben came crashing down around her.

Anna berated herself as she carried her backpack upstairs. I've only known the man for a few weeks and here I am, building my whole life around him. He probably thinks I'm some lovesick teenager. She tossed the pack on the bed in frustration, and practically threw herself into a wing chair in front of the fireplace. She knew she desperately needed a shower, but she was too unhappy to do anything about it at the moment.

Feeling both angry and depressed, Ben was also sitting in front of a fireplace. He hadn't handled the situation with Arianna very well. He should have been honest and told her he was having second thoughts about dating her. The trip back to town had given him too much time to think, making him conscious of the fact others knew he was 'involved' with Arianna. He tried to convince himself that their time in the mountains had been a pleasant interlude, but now it was time to concentrate on decisions needed to be made. There would be little energy remaining to pursue a relationship with Arianna. At least that's what he kept telling himself as he prepared the morning sermon.

Anna, feeling lonely already after only a few hours away

from Ben, spent the rest of the evening reading her Bible. Although they had Bible studies on the camping trip, she felt drawn to the book, knowing it held the power to ease her unhappiness. She began in Psalms, thinking it might sooth her troubled spirit. Before she had even finished the first chapter, she dropped to her knees in front of the fire and prayed, giving all her confusion and unhappiness over to God. When she finally rose, she was exhausted, but content.

After a long soak in the tub, Anna was ready for bed. She snuggled under the covers, wishing she had something to hold to take away the acute loneliness she was feeling. It had been ages since she felt this way, so all alone. Now, with no Ben near and no teens, the darkness around her seemed filled with menace. In her half waking state she felt the darkness swarming around her, like a flock of bats, ready to attack her.

When the phone rang she sat up with a start, her heart pounding in her chest, sweat standing on her brow. She reached for the phone in the darkness, fear making her shake. "Hello," she whispered, her voice quivering.

"Arianna, are you alright?" Ben's concerned tones came over the line. When she didn't answer he became worried. "Arianna, answer me!"

Anna drew in a deep, trembling breath, trying to get herself in control. "I'm here."

"What's wrong?"

She gave a shaky laugh. "I think I was having a nightmare or something. When the phone rang, it must have woken me up."

Ben breathed out in relief. The nagging feeling he had that she was in danger was still present, if a shade less severe. "Are you sure you're all right?" He wanted to offer to come over and comfort her, but knew that he no longer that right. He had just told the woman he wouldn't be able to see her again. When she gave him a mumbled yes, he continued. "I called because I found your camp stove in my stuff. Are you going to need it?" He held his breath, hoping she would say yes, and yet dreading she would.

"No, it's no big deal. I can borrow one from the rafting company." He rang off with a hasty good-bye, and Anna could no longer contain her tears. There must be a reason for his sudden change of attitude, but for the life of her she couldn't figure out why. She didn't think she had done anything to provoke the change. With tears still wet on her cheeks she fell into an exhausted sleep.

Sunday morning Ben searched the congregation for a sign of Arianna, but she was not among the worshipers. He saw Janice McCray sitting in her normal seat, and determined to speak with her after the service. When it was over, he moved quickly in her direction. She saw him coming and waited patiently for him to reach her.

"Good morning, Pastor," she smiled at him.

"Good morning, Janice. I was wondering if Arianna had come this morning."

Janice's smile turned to a slight frown. "No, she didn't. I stopped by her room just before I left, and she was still sleeping. I'm a little worried. She seemed a bit pale to me."

Before he could comment, Ben was approached by the first of his 'appointments'. "I have to go, Janice. Tell Arianna I said hello, and maybe I'll call her later." He knew it seemed strange to Janice, but he wasn't sure how to handle the situation without revealing his uncertainties to the sharp woman.

Janice gave him an assessing glance, but nodded. She drove back to the hotel, deep in prayer for her young Pastor and the young woman who had become like a daughter to her.

Thirteen

The next two days dragged by for Arianna. Not a moment passed that she didn't wish to hear Ben's gentle voice or see his soft gray eyes smiling at her. When Monday and Tuesday went by with no call, she threw herself into her work with a vengeance. Ben's lack of attention hurt more than she was willing to admit, even to herself. The camping trip had given her hope that there might be something special between them, but the time since then had all but dashed those hopes.

By Wednesday morning she had had enough, and drove to West Virginia a day early. The rafting company was delighted to have her for an extra night. Her tour was not scheduled to leave until Thursday afternoon, but the management decided that since Anna was there they would expand the brochure she was scheduled to do to include pictures of the guides as well as some biographical information about each one. Anna had no objections, and set about her task with single minded determination, resolved to forget her sadness.

Ben dropped by McCray House early Wednesday afternoon, hoping to see Arianna. He stopped by the reservation desk in the lobby, and was told by Ella that Janice would like to see him, if he had the time.

"Sure," he replied, and strode down the hall to her apartment.

"Hello, Pastor," she said formally.

Ben wasn't sure how to reply to that, knowing she only used that tone when she was upset with him. She only called him Pastor at church, unless she was teasing or perturbed, and he could tell she wasn't teasing. "Ella said you wanted to have a word with me," Ben began.

"Oh, yes, I did, actually, but was there some other reason you stopped by today?"

Ben fidgeted like a small boy. "Well, I kind of thought I'd see Arianna."

Janice gave him one of her looks, the ones she gave when someone was being particularly annoying or obtuse. "You missed her by about three hours," she informed him tartly.

"What do you mean, missed her? I thought she was leaving tomorrow morning."

"She decided to go early."

Ben inwardly groaned in frustration. Janice was not being very forthcoming with information today. "Did she say why?"

Janice gave him that look again. "Something about being in the way here, was what I gathered. She wasn't talking much."

Her words made Ben feel about two feet tall. He knew his behavior towards her had confused Arianna, but he was confused himself. He hadn't felt comfortable discussing his plans about his future with her, there were just too many variables. But now the process was underway he felt it was safe to resume some type of relationship with Arianna. He just hadn't planned on her leaving before he had a chance to talk to her.

Some of Ben's distress reached Janice, so she took pity on him. "I told her to call you, but obviously she didn't. I have no idea what's going on between the two of you, but I do know that neither of you is happy at the moment."

"There are things I can't discuss with her right now, Janice. I thought she'd at least wait until I could talk to her about everything."

"Ben, for someone as intelligent as you, that was a very foolish thing to do. I've heard you tell us in your sermons that there are some things that just can't wait. I would have thought Arianna was important enough to you that you could have at least told her something of what you're feeling."

"I have told her something," Ben defended himself. "I just don't know if I have the right to pursue a relationship right now."

Janice humphed. "Give me a break, Ben. You're still a man. An unmarried one, I might add. Unless God has told you specifically to remain single, you have the right to pursue a relationship with any God-fearing woman."

Ben, who had been standing this whole time, flung himself in a chair. "Janice, I just don't know. I have always been able to trust you to be discreet. But there are others who are not so discriminating. And for that reason I've had to keep my plans close to the vest, as it were."

The look she gave him was compassionate. "I realize that as a pastor you are under obligation to keep things confidential. But couldn't you have given Arianna a hint of what you're going through? She's a very understanding woman. I don't think she would press you for information she knew you couldn't give her."

Janice started on another tactic. "I know you are a wonderful Pastor, Ben. But I also know you don't belong in a pulpit." At her words, Ben's head jerked up. "Don't look so surprised Ben. I know about the promise you made to Pastor Williams." She knew she had his complete attention now. "I knew your mother very well, Ben. I took care of her when she was ill. She told me all about it."

"Why haven't you said anything before," he wanted to know.

"It's not my business, Ben. It's between you and the Lord."

Ben dropped his head in his hands. All the old pain came rushing to the surface, and tears coursed down his cheeks. He cried for the mother he never got to spend time with and for the woman he now realized he was in love with. One lost through death, and the other through his own stubbornness. He looked up when he felt Janice's hand on his head. Her touch gave him comfort. She never spoke a word, just stood there, a soft smile on her face.

"You remind of my mom, Janice," he said hoarsely, when he could speak.

"Thank you. She was a wonderful woman. And a very wise one." Janice smiled. "Now another very wise woman is telling you that you had better get your act together or you're going to lose one of the most precious gifts God will ever give you."

Ben stood, towering over Janice. He bent down, giving her a soft kiss on the cheek. "Thank you, Janice." He walked out of the room, leaving the woman smiling after him.

At his home later that evening, Ben stood gazing down into the fire blazing in the grate. He had one more meeting, which would take place tomorrow. There was some opposition to his plan, but that was to be expected. If it came to fruition, Jordon Baptist Church would be looking for a new pastor. The people he had taken into his confidence, like Ben himself, wanted only God's will to be done. They had each spent many hours in prayer over the situation, and so far all had been in agreement--Ben was a wonderful pastor, but if God was leading him to step down as their pastor, they would support him.

They also agreed that Ben's reason for stepping down was a worthy one. Ben shared his dream with each one. With the land he had purchased he wanted to open a youth camp, a place where teens from all over could come and experience God's creation. He explained about his own experiences in the mountains of Montana, how he had come to terms with his life and his God. He wanted to share that experience with teenagers, and help them know the Lord on a more personal level.

Ben sighed. His dream was about to come true, but the one person he wanted to share it with wasn't here. And he, himself, had sent her away.

✠✠✠✠✠

Anna spent Wednesday afternoon and Thursday morning photographing and interviewing the guides of the River Rafts. They were a fun group, and she had an enjoyable time learning about them and the work they did. Each of the ten guides had a humorous story to tell about rafting, and some of the trips they had taken. Despite the heaviness in her heart, she was able to laugh over the antics of the group.

On Thursday afternoon when they were getting ready to push off, she looked at the four guides she was to travel with and commented, "I can't believe I'm actually going to let the four of you take me out onto a raging river. I must be out of my mind."

"Ah, come on Anna," one said, "We're not that bad."

She laughed and agreed. "That's true, although, Jesse, if the story you told me yesterday was true, you may be that bad."

Jesse grabbed his chest. "Oh, you wound me!"

As he stumbled around, another guide, Tabitha, casually walked by, giving him a slight push, which sent him right into the river. "Oh, I'm sorry, Jess," she apologized as she gave him a hand out. "I didn't see you standing there."

"Very funny," he griped. The others around began laughing. They completed the loading process, then jumped into the raft, sending it into the river.

The first leg of the journey was the easy trip, the one for beginners. Anna was able to document that part with no problems. There was not a great deal of white water, although there was enough to make it exciting, and to worry Anna about her camera getting wet. She had chosen the non-waterproof one for this trip, and almost regretted it when she came close to falling out of the raft. Jesse had grabbed her just in time.

Anna was terribly embarrassed and knew that her lack of attention was because her thoughts were on Ben when they should have been on what she was doing. She wasn't even sure the pictures she was taking would turn out. I'll just hope for the best, she thought . After that incident, she paid more attention to her work and her comrades, who were having a great time. They were rarely able to go out by themselves, and were making the most of it.

At camp the first night, they sat around the fire sharing stories. To Anna's delight, her four guides were all Christians. They shared their testimonies with her, and she was able to share her's with them. Jesse's story was an especially touching one. He had come to know Christ after his mother's death in an auto accident during his first year of college. Her dying wish had been for him to come to know her Savior, and although it had taken him four years, he had come to know the Lord as his own Savior as well.

"It was such an emotional moment. I was out on the river taking a run with another guy, when the raft tipped over. There was no way we should have survived, but we did. I knew then that it was the Lord. He didn't want me to die without knowing Him. I took the hint, and John was able to lead me to the Lord that night. We had to wait for someone to pick us up, so we were able to talk for ages. I'll always be thankful to John for loving me enough to be blunt with me."

They camped out under the stars that night. Anna stared up into the heavens, glorying that the Lord who had set all that in place loved her even more. "It's so beautiful, Lord," she whispered.

"It sure is," Tabitha whispered back. "What's troubling you, Anna?" Anna glanced sharply over at the girl. Tabitha laughed softly. "You were very distracted today."

Anna grimaced. "Just a little problem with my love life," she joked.

"I know what you mean," Tabitha answered. "Sometimes I think it will take a miracle for the right person to come along."

"It's not the coming along I'm having problems with. I've found him. I thought he felt the same way, but just before this trip, he started acting strangely, as if he were trying to keep something from me. He said he had some things to do and wouldn't be able to call or see me for awhile. I don't know what to do."

Tabitha lay silent for a minute. "I guess you'll just have to trust."

Anna sighed. "I'm trying, but it's not easy."

"It never is."

After they said good night, Anna rolled over, laying her head on her arms, tears falling silently down her cheeks. She was trying to trust, but her heart was breaking anyway.

The next morning they traveled a much more challenging fork of the river. There was no time for Anna to dwell on her problems. The water was higher and rougher than anyone had expected, and it took all their skill to stay upright. Anna was able to snap a few pictures, but it was apparent she would have to be extremely careful.

Over the campfire that night, they discussed their course of action for the next day. Although the sun had been shining for most of the day, the evening sky had turned a leaden gray. "It'll storm before the night is over,"Rod informed them. Even without a weather report it was obvious to everyone that he was right.

Larry, the group leader, broke into the discussion. "Let's wait it out. We're going to have to raft back. There's no way to get us out from this position." The rafters respected Larry's wisdom, since he had been guiding these trips for nearly twenty years.

Rod's prediction was correct. But no one could have predicted the violence of the storm.

Anna felt the first drops about two o'clock in the morning. Not soft drops leading to a gentle shower, but pounding drops, that bespoke of a fierce rain. The others were roused quickly, and the few supplies they had taken out of the raft were packed into waterproof packs. They managed to drag the raft farther up the bank and secure it tightly to a tree, before they dashed to a cleft in the rocks nearby.

"This is not good," Larry shouted above the crashing of the thunder. Tree branches were flying past the opening of their little alcove, illuminated by lightning flashing all around. They were fairly well protected where they were, but the raft was in imminent danger of being blown away along with the tree it was attached to.

The five of them pressed back as far as they could into the opening of the rocks, and at Jesse's prompting they began praying. The storm raged around them for hours. They huddled together for warmth, but there was no escaping the drenching rain. When the storm finally abated the group struggled from their cramped spot to survey the damage. And it was great.

Trees were uprooted, although the one they had attached the raft to had been miraculously spared. Most of their belongs had been blown away or had floated away in the now raging river. It had broken its banks and was swirling almost up to the alcove entrance.

"We have to get out of here," Larry commanded. He glanced up at the sky, which was still dark and menacing. "There's more coming, and it's not safe here."

With grim determination they flipped over the raft before untiing it and pushing it into the swollen river. Anna prayed continuously, both for her safety and that of the others. She had been in dangerous situations before, but always alone. Now there were four other people with her, and it was going to take all five of them working together to escape with their lives.

For hours they paddled furiously, trying to reach their pick up point. When the sky opened and the heavens poured out they were still several miles from where they needed to be. "Faster," Larry screamed above the storm. Despite their exhaustion they pushed their bodies harder and harder.

Finally the cabin that marked the pick up point came into view. Now the problem was how to get to the bank. The river worked against their every movement. They paddled against the current, trying to steer the raft to the side, but to no avail. When the group had just about given up hope of reaching the bank, the river unexpectedly spit the raft out of the water on a huge wave. It floundered for a moment, then dumped its passengers none to gently on the hard ground.

The five of them landed in a heap, with Anna on the bottom. She felt all the air leave her lungs, and was unable to catch her breath. The storm was still raging around them, but Anna couldn't move. Jesse and Rod grabbed her, practically dragging her into the small cabin where the rafting company kept emergency supplies.

"Jeez, guys," Anna gasped, sprawled on the floor, trying to catch her breath. "You're going to have to go on a diet or something."She was still wheezing. Her chest felt like an elephant was sitting on it.

Larry came over to make sure she was all right. "What's the problem?" he asked, crouching down next to her.

"My chest hurts," Anna told him. "I don't think anything is broken. But there's going to be a huge bruise," she complained. He grinned at her, then moved on to the others in the group.

Because of the severity of the storm, it was another hour before they could reach the base camp. Larry was able to assure them that everyone was in good health with just minor cuts and bruises, and they in turn informed the bedraggled fivesome a four wheel drive vehicle would be there in less than an hour. "We sent the truck out after the first storm knowing you would head for the cabin as soon as you could."

By evening the tired rafters were back at the base camp, exhausted but thankful to be safe again. Sitting around the dining room table, they told the camp leader about their experience. Larry told Jim Harris, head of the rafting company, that he believed the river would take several days, perhaps a week before it would be safe to travel on again. Upcoming trips were discussed, and the decision was made to cancel all excursions for the next two weeks.

"Well, Anna, what did you think of our tour?" Jim asked, turning to face her.

She smiled. "It certainly was exciting. I'm not sure how the pictures will turn out, though. I kept getting water in my face." She swung around to look at Jesse, sitting across the table, next to Tabitha. "I wonder how that could have happened?"

Jesse gave her his most innocent look. "I don't know, Anna. I guess you must have been sitting in the wrong spot."

She turned away with a snort. "Seriously though, Jim. The water was too rough to get enough photos of the second trip to make a good brochure. Any chance we could reschedule that part?"

He thought for a moment. "We're booked for the month of July, but we have some openings in August. Could we plan it for then?"

Anna nodded. "That should be fine. I'll work on the beginners brochure in the meantime, and send it out to you. It shouldn't take much longer than two weeks."

She and Jim worked out a timetable for the brochure to be done, then they all headed for their cabins for the night. Anna lay quietly. Now that the excitement had passed, there was too much time to think about Ben. The ache in her heart that she had been able to push into the background during the trip, bubbled up, causing an almost physical pain. Tears slipped silently down her cheeks.

"Oh, Lord," she whispered. "I miss him so much. If he's the man you've chosen for me, please show me. I just don't know." With that prayer, she rolled over and fell asleep, tears still wet on her cheeks.

✠✠✠✠✠

Hundreds of miles away, Ben lay staring up at the ceiling above his bed, his thoughts once more on Arianna. She had been gone three days, six really, since he hadn't seen her since last Saturday night, and he missed her terribly. He was ashamed that he had let his pride affect the way he treated Arianna. And he admitted that it was his pride. He hadn't wanted to tell her about his plans because deep inside he was afraid she might scorn them.

He rolled over, groaning in frustration. There was nothing in her actions that gave any indication that she would laugh at his dream, yet he had been unwilling to take the chance, and had now possibly lost the woman that he had come to love.

Knowing he could not solve this problem, he began to pray, realizing he should have done it much sooner. As he lifted his despair to the Lord, he could feel peace flowing through him, the peace he had been craving all week. It soothed him so much he was finally able to fall into a deep, dreamless sleep.

Fourteen

Anna drove into Jordon Sunday afternoon with a sense of homecoming. Strange, she thought, she never had that feeling in California after returning from an assignment. She smiled as she pulled into her parking spot at McCray House. She was anxious she might Ben, yet desired it so much she could feel her heart pounding just thinking about it.

Sitting back in her sear and closing her eyes, Anna breathed in the scent of the flowers surrounding the parking area. A single tear made its way down her cheek. If she and Ben couldn't resolve their differences, she wouldn't be able to stay here, and that thought caused her a great deal of heartache. She had come to love this town as well as its inhabitants, one in particular.

That was how Ben found her. He had been having lunch with Janice when he heard her jeep pull into the parking lot. I must have it really bad if I can tell her by the sound of her car, he laughed at himself. He walked around the partition between the lot and the patio, and saw Arianna sitting in the front seat with her eyes closed. The top of the Jeep was off, giving him a clear view. The picture she made stopped him in his tracks. Her hair flowed around her shoulders, shining copper in the sunlight. Her face was pale, but the skin was smooth and creamy looking.

As he moved closer, Ben noticed the solitary tear on her cheek, and frowned. He wondered what it could be that was causing her pain, and sighed inwardly. He prayed the culprit wasn't him, although he knew it was a distinct possibility. He reached the door and lay his hand gently on her cheek, brushing the tear away with the pad of his thumb.

Anna thought she was dreaming, and didn't want to open her eyes. Ben's touch on her cheek was so gentle, so loving, it just had to be a dream, and she wasn't ready to end it yet. When the caressing continued, she opened her eyes slightly. Ben was standing at the jeep door, a hesitant smile on his face. In that moment, Anna knew she would forgive him anything if only he would allow her into his life. Love for him was so strong, she was unable to hold back the tears that raced down her cheeks.

Ben opened the door, and pulled her gently from the jeep, drawing her into his arms. She felt so right, so perfect, he was unable to hold back his emotions any longer. He lifted her head and kissed her with all the longing and desperation he had been feeling over the last week.

Anna rose to the challenge, and kissed him back. It was impossible to stop the rush of emotion flowing through her. She loved him so much, and the time away from him had only strengthened those feelings. Her arms roped around his neck pulling his head even closer.

Both of them were breathless when they finally broke apart. Ben looked down into her dark brown eyes, and saw all the love he had been longing for. "I should apologize for that," he whispered softly in her ear. "But I won't. I love you, Arianna," Ben admitted with a sigh. He took her lips again, this time gently, almost reverently, causing her legs to buckle. Ben held her tightly against him, laying his cheek on top of her head.

As much as she wanted him to hold her, her bruised ribs protested at the rough treatment. He was holding her close to his heart, and as tight as he could, almost as if he were afraid she might disappear. When he tightened the embrace even more she couldn't hold back a soft moan of pain.

Ben quickly loosened his hold, looking sharply at her face. He wasn't prepared for the grimace of pain he saw. "What's wrong?"

Not wanting to be out of his arms, Anna snuggled against his chest, wrapping her arms around his waist. "We had a little bad weather on the rafting trip. I got caught at the bottom of the pile in the rush to get to the cabin. I didn't break anything, but those guys are huge."

He muddled through her explanation but got caught by the word 'guys'. "What guys?" Ben snapped, a frown on his face. His look turned sheepish when she glanced up in surprise at his tone. "Sorry, I know I shouldn't even ask that question after the way I've treated you. Are you badly hurt?"

Anna smiled. Ben almost sounded jealous. Well, she wouldn't keep him in suspense. The last thing she wanted was another misunderstanding between them. "No, I'm not badly hurt. Just bruised. And 'those guys' are the rafting company guides. I should have said 'those people' since there was a woman among them." Her voice was muffled, but he heard the light teasing note in it and gave a chagrined grin.

"All right, I deserve a lot worse than what you're giving me." He was silent for a moment then spoke in a hushed voice. "I'm sorry, Arianna. I should not have treated you that way. Can you ever forgive me?"

She looked up into his face and smiled. "Of course, I'll forgive you, if you'll forgive me for going off in a huff without talking to you first." She backed out of his arms, and took his hand. "If you have a minute or two, why don't you come in and I'll tell you about my trip. Then you can tell me what it is that's been on your mind," she added, referring to his abrupt behavior during the previous week.

They walked hand in hand through the lobby. Janice, standing in the door of her apartment, saw them and smiled to herself. Well, ladies, she thought, as she stared heavenwards, I've done what I could to make sure your children are happy. They're on their own now.

Up in her room, Ben made himself comfortable on one of the chairs in front of the fireplace, while Anna sat crossed legged on her bed. "The first day was fun," she told him. "There were four guides and myself, and we started on the beginners tour. We had a great time. Since they aren't able to get out alone often, they made sure they made the most of it." Anna went on to tell him some of the antics the four friends pulled on each other. "I didn't want to intrude on their fun, and I had a lot on my mind anyway." She glanced over at Ben, and he was in no doubt that his behavior was what she was thinking about.

"Jesse saved me from a dunking. I wasn't paying attention and almost fell in, camera and all. He felt that I owed him, so of course I had to help him with his next prank." Anna paused for a minute. "I wasn't sure it would be the best thing to do, but I went along. He wanted to get Tabitha back for pushing him in the river earlier in the day, so while she was talking with me, he quietly slipped into our tent and filled her sleeping bag with pine cones. I felt it my duty as a female to let her know.

"Later that evening after we were all in bed, I heard the loudest scream I have ever heard. It seems Tabitha one upped Jesse. Instead of pine cones, she had filled his bag with itching powder. Where she got it, I have no idea." Anna grinned mischievously. Ben looked at her doubtfully, wondering if she actually could have done something so awful to a member of his sex. The gleam in her eye gave him his answer. He knew without a doubt who had supplied the powder.

"So what did the poor man do?" he asked, thinking to himself that if he was going to date this woman he would have to keep on his toes.

"Oh, he took a little dip in the creek. We had an extra sleeping bag, so we let his air out overnight." The laughter in her eyes dimmed to be replaced with something close to fear. "The next evening the weather changed." She didn't add any more and Ben looked at her curiously. Her face was turned toward the window, so he couldn't see her expression.

During the silence, he thought over the past few days.Understanding dawned in his eyes. She had been in West Virginia. The news had been filled with stories of the tornadoes and torrential rain that had passed through that state. "How bad?" he asked, almost afraid to hear.

"Bad enough," was her cryptic reply. "I lost everything I brought with me, expect my small camera bag." Anna sighed. "I don't think I have ever been so frightened in my life. We hid in the cleft of a rock formation. If it weren't for the Lord's protection, I don't think we would have made it back. The river didn't want to let us go."

Ben walked over to where Anna was sitting on the bed and hauled her as gently as he could into his arms. Arianna hadn't given him all the details, but he could fill in a lot by himself, and he knew it was only by God's grace that she was here. If something had happened to her he wasn't sure what he would have done, but the Lord had given him the opportunity to make up for his mistakes. He would not let her go again.

"You haven't lost anything, Arianna," he told her softly. "When I came to see you on Wednesday and Janice told me you had already left, I was hurt and angry that you hadn't called me. She diplomatically pointed out that I have ten fingers and a phone, and could have made time to speak with you. I'm sorry, Arianna. I'm sorry for all the hurt and pain I've caused." Ben bent his head and kissed her softly.

When Anna opened her eyes, Ben was smiling down at her. "You haven't lost everything, you know. I still have your camp stove." His joking remark lifted her dark spirits, and for the first time in a long time she laughed with abandon.

When she was finally able to speak, she said, "I know I haven't lost everything, Ben. The Lord will always be with me, no matter what happens. It took me awhile to learn that, but it's a lesson I plan never to forget." She smiled sweetly up at him. "Now, maybe you should tell me what's going on in your life."

Ben hesitated, not because he didn't want to tell her, but because beneath that sweet smile Arianna was hiding exhaustion. Her face was very pale, and her brown eyes didn't have their normal sparkle. "Not now, sweetheart," he told her softly. When she looked at him in confusion, he smiled tenderly. "You've been through a lot the last couple of days, and you need to rest." When Arianna made to protest, he hushed her by putting his finger over her lips. "Yes, you do. You're white as a ghost and shaking. I promise to tell you, but it's a long story. Let's just relax tonight, and tomorrow I'll take you on a picnic, and we'll talk. All right?"

As much as she wanted to share Ben's problems, Anna realized the wisdom of his words. She was very tired, and still in some pain, and knew she couldn't give Ben the attention he deserved. So she reluctantly agreed.

"I knew you would see it my way," he kidded her. Before she could make a comment, Ben continued. "Are you hungry?"

"Maybe a little," she answered.

"I'll go down and make you a snack," he volunteered. She nodded her agreement, and he left the room.

Anna settled back on the bed, putting pillows behind her. She hadn't realized just how tired she was. I'll just close my eyes for a minute, she told herself. Before she knew it, she was sound asleep.

Ben had a feeling something like that would happen. When he came back upstairs, it was to find Arianna curled up against the pillows, fast asleep. He set the tray he was carrying down on the bedside table, and, getting a blanket, carefully covered her. He looked down at her, heart overflowing with the love he was feeling. Not wanting to leave her again, he brought one of the chairs by the bed and settled into it.

I don't want to lose her, Lord, he prayed silently. Please help me find the words to tell her how much she means to me. Ben's prayers lasted for some time, before he, too, dozed off. When he woke, the room was dark. He reached over and turned on the bedside lamp. It cast a rosy hue over the immediate area. He glanced down at Arianna, still sleeping peacefully. The light reflected off her shiny, copper hair. Ben reached out to touch it, enjoying the soft and silky feel of it between his fingers.

"Oh, Arianna," he whispered. She stirred slightly, and opened her eyes. Ben became lost in the dark brown depths. He ran his fingers through her silky hair, and smiled tenderly. "I love you, Arianna. So much that it frightens me."

Ben's whispered words caused tears to come to her eyes.

They so closely resembled her own feelings. She reached up and ran a finger down his cheek. “I know how you feel,” she answered quietly. Sitting up, she swung her legs over the side of the bed so she was facing him. “I’ve never felt this way before, Ben. I don’t know how to react to it. One minute I’m soaring like an eagle, the next I’m frightened as a mouse being chased by a cat. It definitely isn’t good for the ole ticker, here.” Anna placed her hand over her heart. Although her words were joking, both she and Ben knew the truth behind them.

“Well, we will just have to do something about that,” he promised. “But now it’s time for me to go.” Anna stared at him in confusion. “It’s late, sweetie. I have to prepare a few things for a meeting tomorrow morning, but tomorrow afternoon I’m free. I’ll pick you up about one. We can have a late lunch and talk. You should be more awake then,” he teased.

Anna gave a guilty smile. Despite the nap she had just taken, her body was telling her it wanted much, much more. She rose when Ben did, and walked with him to the door. “Ben,” she said. He stopped and turned to look at her. She looked up into his face. “I just wanted to tell you how much I love you.”

Ben grinned. His heart felt so light and carefree he was almost afraid. “I love you too, Arianna. Never before, never like this.” He bent to kiss her lightly on the lips. “Now, I really have to go.” When Anna made to follow him out into the hall, he forestalled her. “No, you don’t have to see me out. Go eat the snack I left, then go back to bed. Just don’t sleep too late,” he warned her jokingly.

Anna remembered on the camping trip when she had slept until one in the afternoon. “I promise not to, although after the last few days, leaving that comfortable bed will be hard.” She grinned saucily up at Ben. “But I guess you’re worth it.”

“How kind of you to think so.” With a quick peck on the cheek, Ben sauntered down the hall. He turned at the top of the stairs. “I’ll see you tomorrow.”

When Ben disappeared around the turn in the stairs, Anna

went back into her room. The smile on her face threatened to stretch her skin beyond endurance, but she couldn't hold it back. She had just sat down to eat, when there was a knock on her door. "Come in," she called, knowing it was going to be Janice.

"Welcome back, stranger," Janice greeted her happily. "No need to ask how things are between you and Ben," she commented, noting Anna's high color and smiling face. "Ben looked just about the same as you."

Anna giggled, unable to hold back her happiness. Janice sat down across the small table. "It's good to see you happy again, Anna, dear. Ben, too, for that matter. He was moping around like he'd lost his best friend." She picked up a carrot stick, and began munching. "So what is going on between the two of you?" Janice was noted for her forthrightness.

"I love him," Anna stated.

"No kidding," Janice snorted. "Like I didn't know that. I mean, what's next?"

Anna looked at her. "I don't know, Janice. Ben and I need to talk. He still hasn't told me what's been bothering him. He's picking me up tomorrow at one for lunch. Maybe I'll find out then." She turned her head away to hide a grin. "When I do, you'll be the first to know."

"I should hope so," Janice retorted. "I've been praying long and hard for the two of you. I'd like to move on to something else. So get it together, will you?"

They munched on, making small talk. Anna relegated Janice with tales of her trip, downplaying the danger she had been in. Janice laughed at the stories of the guides, and especially when she found out Anna had provided the itching powder.

It was over an hour later when Janice took her leave. Anna took a long soak in the tub, scenting the water with lilacs, then, wrapped in her silk robe, she stepped out onto the balcony of her room. From her vantage point she could see hundreds of stars in the sky, and the moon coming up over the horizon, huge and bright. Oh Father, she prayed, thank you so much for Ben, and for his love. Thank you for answering my prayers, and bringing us together. Her prayers were interrupted by the phone ringing.

"Hello," she answered, expecting to hear Ben's gentle voice greeting her.

"Where have you been?" Lance's agitated voice came over the line. His tone was harsh when he continued. "I told you to come home, and I meant now."

Anna was almost too shocked to reply, but only almost. "Hello, Lance, its so nice to hear from you," the sarcasm in her voice would have made anyone else cringe, but Lance was past caring.

"Don't give me that. When will you be here?"

"Lance," Anna said, trying very hard to be patient. "I'm not coming back. I've decided to stay in Jordon indefinitely."

"What?!" his voice shrieked over the line. Anna had to hold the phone away from her ear. "You have to come back." His voice sounded almost desperate.

"Well, no I don't, Lance. I told you before I left that I don't want to see you any more."

"But I want to see you. You can't just drop me like that."

Anna sighed. "We don't have the same values, Lance. We never have. I don't want just an affair with a man, I want a husband who will love me more than himself. You know that would never be the case with you. And I don't love you."

Lance's muttered curse came over the line quite clearly. He obviously wasn't happy about the outcome of this call, but there was no way Anna could make it any easier. She didn't want to tell him about Ben. That would probably send him ballistic, and he was angry enough already.

"I'm coming out there, Anna," Lance informed her bluntly. "You can't treat me this way. I need to see you."

"Please, don't Lance. Nothing will change."

Lance either didn't hear her, which wasn't likely, or was choosing to ignore her comment, which was more probable. "I'll be out within a few days, Anna. Expect me." With that he hung up.

Anna sat staring at the phone in disbelief. She didn't want to face Lance, was actually afraid to. The memory of the last time they had seen each other was still fresh in her mind. He would have raped her if the alcohol he had been drinking hadn't affected his coordination. Just the thought of confronting him made her tremble.

When the phone rang again, a minute later, she jumped. The trembling increased, and she was afraid to answer. It rang six times before she finally picked it up. She made no sound, just held the receiver gingerly next to her ear.

"Hello. Is anyone there?" Ben's reassuring voice floated around her. The warm sound of it affected her so much she burst into tears. "Anna? What's wrong?" She couldn't answer through her sobs. "Anna!"

"I'm sorry," she sobbed. "I'm sorry!" She dropped the phone and threw herself on the bed, trying desperately to stem the flow of tears.

She was still trying twenty minutes later when Ben rushed into her room, closely followed by Janice. The tears coursed down her cheeks, and her body was trembling uncontrollably. "Arianna," Ben's voice came from a distance. "Can you hear me?" One hand rested on the small of her back, the other ran gently through her hair. "Speak to me, sweetheart, please." He turned to Janice. "Janice, she seems to be in shock. Can you bring some hot coffee up here?" When she left, he turned back to Arianna.

"I'm sorry," Anna mumbled into the pillow she was clutching. "I don't know what's wrong with me."

Ben reached down, pulling her into a sitting position so he could see her face. It was white, setting off her huge brown eyes. His heart broke at the sight. He didn't say a word, just took her in his arms. Tenderly brushing the hair out of her face, he gave her a loving smile. "You're exhausted, Arianna. Just relax, let me hold you." He did just that.

Soon, the trembling subsided, and Anna was able to speak. "Lance called." The words came out bluntly, so much so that Ben loosened his hold to stare down at her face. What he saw worried him. She was afraid, and trying to hide it.

"What did he want?"

Anna shuddered. "He's coming out here. He says he has to see me." She looked into Ben's eyes. "I told him not to. He was so angry, Ben."

Ben drew her close. "I won't let him hurt you, Arianna." Janice entered just then with the coffee. She gave the cup to Ben, who held it for Arianna. "Take a sip of this," he commanded softly. She sipped obediently.

Janice looked over her head at Ben. "What's wrong?" she inquired. Ben shook his head. The woman nodded, and glanced down at Arianna. "She's asleep."

Ben gently laid Anna on the bed, covering her with the quilt. "I called Doc, and he told me to put one of my sleeping pills in it," Janice informed him. "He said he'd drop by if we needed him to."

"I don't think that will be necessary. I think the stress of Lance calling and the raft trip just caught up with her." He bent down to kiss Anna's cheek. When he rose, he informed Janice, "I'll be staying the night. Is there a room close by?"

"Sure. Next door is empty." She left to prepare it, and Ben sat down in the bedside chair. "Oh, Lord," he prayed out loud. "Bring your peace to Arianna. Take away her fear, Lord, and give me the strength to protect her from any harm." He prayed for awhile more, then left silently to retire to the room next door.

Fifteen

Ben woke early the next morning, knowing there was much to do. The first was to call Richard Weston, head of the board of Jordon Baptist Church. Ben was scheduled to met with him at ten o'clock this morning, but planned to cancel. Ben's decision to leave the church, although not public yet, was final. He had planned to tell Richard this morning in person, but due to the circumstances, would just do it over the phone. Richard could always come to McCray House if he needed to talk to Ben.

After showering and dressing, Ben slipped over to Anna's room. He knocked quietly on the door, but when he didn't receive an answer, he opened it silently. Anna was still cuddled on the bed, sleeping peacefully, for which Ben was thankful. He had been woken twice last night by Arianna's screams. She had been having nightmares, Ben was certain, but Anna had thankfully never woken up. Ben had managed to calm her while she was still sleeping, which was good for her, but he was exhausted.

His thoughts were interrupted when Doc Watson came through the door. "Hello, young man," he greeted Ben softly. "How is our young lady this morning?"

Ben shook the older man's hand. "What are you doing here so early?" he wanted to know.

"Had to deliver a baby early, so I thought I'd drop by. I was kind of worried when Janice told me about Anna. Did the sleeping pill do the trick?"

"Yes, thankfully. I think she's all right. I know she had some close calls while she was rafting this past week, and then she had a rather frightening phone call. I think her emotions just finally caught up with her," Ben explained. "Her face was so pale last night. That had me worried, but she looks all right this morning."

Doc went over to stand by the bed. He gently took Anna's wrist in his hand, and took her pulse. "Did she sleep all right?"

"She had a couple of nightmares, but she never woke up," Ben answered.

"Her wrist looks bruised," Doc noticed, setting her hand down on the quilt. "Do you know why?"

Ben thought for a moment. "Arianna said she ended up on the bottom of a pile of people running for shelter in a storm during her trip. It's possible it could be from that. She told me her ribs were bruised because of it."

Doc frowned. "Well, I don't want to wake her. The pill should probably keep her out most of the morning. I'll check on her later." The two men went out into the hall. "If it is just emotional exhaustion, she should be fine later in the day. Keep me posted, will you, Ben."

"Sure, Doc." Doc Watson left. Ben went back into the room.

Janice came up a short time later with a breakfast tray. "Doc said she should be fine," she said as she laid the tray down.

"Thanks, Janice. Yeah, she should be. I'll be happier when she wakes up and tells me herself." He pulled up to the table and began eating.

"She'll be up soon, Ben. Until then you'll just have to be patient. A good quality to have for a husband."

Ben's head jerked up, and his startled gray eyes met Janice's twinkling blue ones. "I see a lot more than people give me credit for," she told Ben. "I wouldn't wait too long, though. She might get frustrated and send you packing just to annoy you."

He grinned. "I'll give your advice some thought, Janice. Any other words of wisdom you want impart?"

"No. I'm sure you can handle it from now on." Janice looked at him sternly. "But don't mess up again. I don't think she can handle much more." With that she swept out of the room, leaving Ben staring after her.

When Ben finished his breakfast, he called Richard Weston to finalize his decision to leave the church. Richard was disappointed to loose a wonderful pastor, but delighted that Ben's plan for the youth camp would be completed in just over a week. "We should be able to have our first camp next spring," Ben told the man.

"That's great, Ben. I'm sorry to see you leave the pulpit, but your camp will be a great asset to the church and the community. I have to admit you have a great way with the youth. Let me know if you need any help," Richard offered, then hung up.

With that out of the way, Ben was able to devote all of his time to watching the woman he loved sleeping. He also used the time to pray about their future together, and the future of the youth camp. In the midst of his prayers he heard Anna stirring, and he opened his eyes to see her staring up at him.

"Good morning, sweetheart," he whispered, bending down to tenderly kiss her.

"You live dangerously, Ben," Anna said softly. He looked at her in confusion, and she giggled. "Kissing a woman with morning breath could do a person in," she teased.

He laughed. "I'll just have to take that chance because I can't seem to control the urge to kiss you, no matter what time of day." He smiled down at her. "How are you feeling?"

Anna lifted her hand to run her fingers through her tangled hair. "I don't know. I feel kind of funny, like my head is full of cotton."

"That's probably from the sleeping pill Janice slipped into your coffee last night," Ben explained.

"Why would she do that?" Anna wondered.

Ben gave her a questioning glance. "Don't you remember what happened last night?"

She shook her head. "I'm not sure. I remember talking to you." She blushed. When Ben saw it, he grinned. "Don't let it go to your head," she told him smartly. "You told me to eat and get a good night's sleep, because you were going to take me out to lunch so we could talk." Anna looked over at the bedside clock which read eleven-thirty. "Why are you here now?"

Ben wasn't sure what to tell her, but knew she would remember sooner or later. "You had a phone call from Lance last night," he reminded her.

Anna's face went pale. "That's right," she whispered. For a minute Ben thought she might faint, but then her color returned to normal. "He said he had to see me, and he was coming out here." She waved a hand in the air. "I told him not to, but he never did listen very well. I guess I kind of snapped."

"That's a nice way to put it," Ben commented.

A blush spread over Anna's face. "I'm sorry, Ben. After you left everything just seemed to come at me. You telling me you didn't want to see me any more, the rafting trip, then you telling me you loved me." The blush became darker. "I was so tired, and then Lance called. All I could remember was the last time we had seen each other, and it scared me." She looked up at Ben, who was scowling. "But Lance can't hurt me, Ben. Admittedly, he sounded really angry, but as long as he hasn't been drinking, I'm sure he wouldn't hurt me physically."

"He won't be hurting you physically, because you won't be seeing him unless I'm here, Arianna. Is that clear?"Ben's voice was stern and unyielding. Anna was surprised that he would take that tone of voice with her, until she realized that he was afraid for her.

"Don't worry, Ben," she assured him. "I won't see him alone." She reached for his hand. "I love you, Benjamin Thompson."

"And don't you forget it, Arianna Jenkins," he growled as he took her in his arms. He let her go a moment later. "Now take a long, hot shower, and get dressed. We're going out to lunch, and then back to my house. I really need to talk to you."Although his words were serious, his tone was light, as though he were excited about what he was going to share with her.

Ben exuberance gave Anna the lift she needed to start the day. Her shower, although hot, was quick, and she dressed hurriedly, because she wanted nothing more than to be back in Ben's arms. She rushed down the stairs to find Ben on the lobby phone.

"Sure, I can make it, but push it back until seven, all right. I have something to do that won't wait." He nodded his head, mumbled a time or two, then said good-bye. He turned and saw Anna staring at him. "I have to go out of town later this afternoon," he said bluntly. "But I want us to talk now, and I know you are probably starving." He grinned. "I know I am," he whispered in her ear. Anna blushed to the roots of her hair and Ben laughed. "Don't worry, sweetie. I won't leave you again without telling you what's going on."

He took her arm and led her out to his truck. "I'll make something at home so we can talk while you eat." The ride out to his farm was quiet. Anna didn't know what to say, and Ben didn't want to say anything until they were in the comfort and privacy of his home.

When he sat a plateful of eggs, bacon, and hash browns in front of her, Anna was positive she would never be able to eat. She was as nervous as a kitten, afraid that Ben would tell her he had decided against their relationship. She pushed the food around on her plate until Ben finally took the fork from her and began to feed her himself.

"You have to eat Arianna," he commanded. "I know you think I'm going to tell you I don't want to see you again, and I don't blame you considering what happened the last time. But there isn't anything farther from the truth." He set the fork down, and took her chin in his rough palm. "I love you, and I always will. Even though I have to leave soon, I intend to be back within a day or two. And before I leave I want to assure you that I will be back."

He looked down into her confused face. "There are things I want to say to you that there won't be time for now, but know this. I love you." He emphasized each word with a powerful kiss.

"I can tell you this, though. I've decided to step down as pastor of the church."

Anna turned shocked eyes to him. "What! You can't do that, Ben!"

"It wasn't a decision I made lightly, Arianna. There were definite reasons behind it. When I accepted the pastor position I did it because I felt Pastor Williams had wanted me to. When he told me to take his place so many years ago, I thought he meant as leader of the church. I thought there was no way I could do that, but when I decided to go into the ministry, that all changed. And then I was offered Jordon Baptist Church, the church that Pastor Williams had lead. I felt it was of the Lord. And it was. It got me back to Jordon.

"When I first accepted Christ, I had this great desire to share Him with my friends. I felt compelled to do it. As I grew, so did the desire to lead others to Christ. I started by helping with the youth group in my church in Montana. When I went to seminary it was with thoughts of being a youth pastor. But then the letter came asking me to take the church here. I thought to myself, maybe this is what I'm suppose to do. So I put my dreams of helping the youth aside and took the church."

Ben rose, went to the sink and poured himself a glass of water. Drinking some, he set the glass down. "I was wrong. Pastor Williams hadn't been asking me to take over his flock, he was telling me to take his place as a Christian, and to lead others the way he had lead me. By example, by doing what I knew best. And what I know best is how to relate to teen-agers."

Anna was momentarily stunned. When he first started talking Anna thought for sure he was going to tell her that although he loved her, her faith was too weak to work with him in the church, and he would have to end their relationship. Now he was telling her that he had been wrong in his calling. It was difficult for her to put it all together.

Ben looked at Anna and smiled. Confusion was written

plainly on her beautiful face. He could almost see the wheels turning in her head. "All those meetings I've been having, all the thinking I had to do. It all relates to my decision to leave the pastorate and head a youth camp."

Anna was more confused than ever. What youth camp? As far as she knew there wasn't one in the immediate area, and considering what she knew about Ben, Anna was certain he intended to stay in this area. She cocked her head at Ben waiting for him to continue.

He walked back over to the table and took up the fork again. "Open wide," he teased, as he lifted a forkful of food to her mouth. Out of reflex she opened her mouth. Ben slid the fork in, and Anna chewed mechanically. "That's a good girl."

One thing that Anna absolutely hated was being patronized, and she could tell Ben was doing just that. Her brown eyes grew fierce. She finished chewing the food in her mouth and was just about to let him have it when Ben spoke.

"It's about time!"Anna's mouth hung open unattractively, and she snapped it shut. "I have never known you to be so blah, Arianna. I was beginning to worry."

Anna glared at him, still annoyed. "You're lucky I didn't wap you one. I've had more excitement over the last four days then I've had over most of my adult life. I'm not at my best."

"I know," Ben soothed. "But I wanted to make sure you were taking everything in."

"Let me review, Ben," Anna said testily. "In the mountains you tell me you love me. We come down and you tell me you can't see me any more, at least for awhile. I leave, almost getting killed on a rafting trip. I come back and you tell me you love me. The next day you tell me you have to leave.Am I getting it so far?" she snapped.

Ben laughed. "Yeah, I guess that's right so far." Anna wasn't taking his teasing well, he could tell, but she was so pretty with her cheeks flushed he just couldn't help pushing her a little farther. "Please continue."

Eyes becoming dangerously dark, Anna went on. "You practically force feed while telling me you've decided to step down as pastor of your church, to do what I have no idea."

"That's right so far. Now let me go on." Ben took her arm and led her outside. Lifting his hand to encompass the whole area, he said, "The one thing I want most in the world is to help youth learn the truth about the Lord. This land is full of God's creation. I plan to open a youth camp, here, for teens all over the country."

Anna's eyes opened wide, comprehension dawning. "That's wonderful, Ben!" she enthused. "You're wonderful with them."

"That's why I have to go to Williamsburg this afternoon. My financing has come through and the company that's sponsoring the camp would like me to come in and make a presentation to its board."

Throwing herself into his arms, Anna almost knocked Ben off his feet. He recovered nicely, wrapping his arms around her. "I know you'll be fantastic," she told him.

Gray eyes gleaming, Ben pulled her tight against him. "I have to leave soon, but there were other things I planned to say to you today." He looked down into her face. "Will you wait?"

"Of course. I'm sorry for running off last time."

"Don't apologize, Arianna. You shouldn't have been put in that situation in the first place. I'm the one who's sorry." He gave her a lingering kiss. "When I get back we'll have a lot of time to talk properly. Until then, can you do me a favor?" he asked.

"Sure."

"Think about me," Ben whispered, his mouth descending.

When Anna was able to think again, she wondered who he was kidding. She thought about him constantly. "I guess I can do that," she teased softly, reaching up to kiss his chin. "I might even spend more than fifty seconds a minute doing it."

Ben had to think about that one first, then he grinned.

They walked back into the house, and talked about trivial things while Ben packed for his trip. When he was done, he drove Anna back to the hotel, and with a jaunty wave, drove off.

Anna stood on the front lawn until she couldn't see him any more, then went up to her room. She was so excited about Ben's youth camp. It would be a great place for teens to come. Maybe I'll get a little brochure together while he's gone, Anna thought as she changed from her jeans into shorts and t-shirt.

The weather had warmed up considerably in the last hour. The spring had been cold and wet, and early summer had also been rather chilly, but now it was really beginning to feel like summer. Which was only right since it was the end of June. Anna started at the thought. It was already the end of June. She sighed in relief. The last group of pictures for *Whispering Wilds* had been sent off to Lauren just before Anna had left for the rafting trip. That project was now completed, and she could turn her talents to other things.

She had to finish the beginners brochure for the rafting company, and take more pictures for the book about Jordon, but the brochure was practically done anyway, and taking pictures around town was such an enjoyable experience, Anna never counted it as work. This is going to be a great summer, Anna smiled broadly. She threw a few extra canisters of film into her backpack, along with her camera and rushed down the stairs. In the kitchen she was just wrapping the last cookie and stuffing them into the bag when Janice came in.

"Hello, dear," she said, cast clanking against the tile floor. "Going somewhere?"

"Sure am," Anna answered brightly. "I'm going on a hike."

Janice looked at her for a moment, then grinned. "You seem much better, this afternoon," she commented. "Any special reason?"

"No, just in a mood to work. See ya," she called, as she strode happily out of the room.

Shaking her head, Janice watched with a smile."Ah, love," she said softly, turning to get herself a cup of coffee from the pot on the stove.

Anna jumped into the jeep and drove out to Ben's house. For the next three hours, she hiked over the land, snapping away. Every once in awhile she paused to write down some ideas in her notebook. She ended up at the creek where Ben had found her asleep so long ago, it seemed, her feet resting in the cold water. I won't have that problem today, Anna thought. She was sweating heavily, the air around her hot and muggy.

Brushing perspiration off her face with the sleeve of her shirt, Anna bent down and took off her hiking boots and socks. She dipped her feet in the cold water, smiling at the small fish trying to nip her toes. "Easy does it fellas," she said. She splashed some of the cool water over her face. She swished her feet around for a few more minutes, then moved to lean up against a nearby tree.

For another hour she sat there, in the peace of the woods, and prayed. Never in her life had she felt this light-hearted, and she knew it was more than her love for Ben that was making her feel this way. Sitting there, lifting her face to heaven, she thanked the Lord for the beautiful day He had given her. Despite the suddenly oppressive heat, she had never felt so wonderful. Anna was able to push her fears and doubts aside and let the Lord fill her heart.

It was getting dark when Anna returned to the hotel. Janice, concerned about the hour, was waiting in the lobby for her. "I was getting worried, dear," she chastened Anna.

"Sorry, Janice. I lost track of time. It's so peaceful in the woods."

"And what woods might that be?" she teased."It wouldn't be because they're Ben's woods, would it?"

"Any woods would have done," Anna said haughtily, a gleam in her eye.

"Well, I have dinner ready for you," Janice told her. The

two women ate a hearty dinner in Janice's apartment. Anna told her what she was planning as a surprise for Ben, which the other woman thought was a great idea.

"That's a terrific thing to do, Anna."

"I think Ben's doing a terrific thing. I want to help in some small way."

Janice had a few ideas of her own to add. The women tossed ideas around until almost mid-night when Janice finally told Anna she had to go to bed. "You'll get exhausted again, dear, and I don't think Ben will take kindly to me keeping you up so late."

"It was worth it, Janice, but I am kind of tired. I'll see you in the morning." She went to her room, skipping happily up the stairs. Although excited about her day, she was asleep almost as soon as her head touched the pillow.

The next day was almost an exact duplicate of the day before, except that Ben called early that morning to let Anna know there was a hold up in Williamsburg. One of the board members had an emergency, and wouldn't be able to attend the meeting, so it had been postponed one day.

"That's not so bad in itself. I can use the extra time to get some shopping done. But it means I won't be home for at least two days."

He sounded so sad, Anna had to smile. "Don't worry. I'll hang around." She snapped her fingers. "You could do me a favor while you're there," she informed him. When he asked what it was she told him about the camping store she had found.

"I lost a lot of equipment on the rafting trip. My sleeping bag, some cooking utensils, and my climbing gloves. Could you go there and get me some replacements?"

"Wouldn't you rather do that yourself?" he asked. "I'm not sure I'll get the right stuff."

"Oh, don't worry. The store has a list of what I have. When I was there a few weeks ago, they put it in the computer. It shouldn't take too long. That way I don't have to make another trip out there."

"Well, in that case, I will. Anything to keep you in Jordon." His voice had a smile in it. "I have to go, sweetie. Richard is waving frantically in my direction. I'll call you tomorrow."

With the whole day stretching in front of her, Anna went to work. The brochure for the rafting company was done in less than two hours. She walked into town and sent it via overnight mail to Jim, knowing he would be pleased. It had come out exceptionally well, although Anna was still disappointed that she had not been able to do the other runs.

While in town, Anna spoke to some of the older residents. They were gathered, as usual at the small general store, talking, playing checkers, and just enjoying the warmth of the day. Happy to answer her questions about the town, they often reminisced about what Jordon was like years ago. Anna, a small tape recorder in hand, sat with the older people, soaking in the stories of days gone by, days when her mother and grandparents had lived in this town. Quite a few of them knew her grandparents, and her mother as a young woman. The stories they told Anna showed how much the Millers had cared for their daughter and how much it had hurt them when Jackie had left town with a man from California.

Anna knew that Jackie had made her peace with her parents. It had just been monetarily impossible for them to see each other. Jackie had been practically living in poverty most of Anna's younger years, and when they could afford to go back to Jordon, the Millers were both dead. It made Anna happy to know that her grandparents had been well thought of by the community.

Back at McCray House later that evening, Anna sat at the desk, thinking about all that had happened in the last few months. Looking back she could see the Lord's hand moving her to where she was now, in Jordon, once again in His hands. She was still mulling over the changes in her life when the phone rang.

"Don't hang up on me," Lance commanded.

Anna was startled, but was determined not to let Lance

frighten her again. "I won't hang up Lance. But before you say any more, let me tell you that I have no intention of seeing you again."

"We'll see about that," he sneered.

His words were slightly slurry, so Anna knew he had been drinking. She was worried about that. He was drinking way too much, had been for quite awhile. "You should stop drinking," she told him.

His reply was quite harsh, and left Anna speechless. What was wrong with him, she wondered. Even in his most obnoxious moments Lance had never been so infuriated with her, and considering how many times she had refused him, there had been many times when he was upset.

"I'll be there tomorrow afternoon," he informed her, his voice ragged. "Make sure you're around."Before she could reply, he hung up. Anna stared at the phone in disbelief. He'd be here tomorrow. Ben wouldn't be back for several days. What was she going to do?

Sixteen

The morning brought no revelations to Anna about what to do with Lance. After a night of broken sleep, interrupted by constant nightmares, Anna had awakened at five and decided she might as well get up. Morning was a time she used to pray for the upcoming day, and Anna knew she had much praying to do this morning if she was going to be seeing Lance this afternoon. If he had been speaking the truth he would be in Jordon in less than twelve hours, and she still wasn't sure how to handle it. Ben had not left his hotel number with her, thinking, of course, that it wouldn't be necessary. She would have to take care of this problem by herself.

Taking a seat out on her balcony, Anna noticed that even at this early hour it was already hot and steamy. Although she hadn't heard the weather report it was undoubtedly going to storm sometime today. The air was heavy with moisture but Anna paid no heed. She propped her Bible in her lap and began reading in the Psalms, her usual habit when she was bothered by something. The words soothed her troubled spirit, and by the time the sun was peeking over the horizon, Anna felt much more able to deal with the upcoming day.

Anna showered and dressed in a comfortable combed cotton dress she had purchased the last time she was in Williamsburg. It flattered her trim figure, and the dark green color set off her auburn hair. Ben had complimented her on her 'fine taste in clothes', telling her that he liked her in the outfit. Anna just considered it a knocking around dress, when she didn't feel like wearing shorts.

Before she left her room Anna picked up her backpack and threw in a couple of changes of clothes. She had no intention of waiting around for Lance, and would spend the day wandering around Ben's property. The weather was so warm, she had a feeling she might want to take a swim in the creek before returning that afternoon. She also took her camera case, always on the lookout for a good shot.

Janice was not around when Anna left McCray House, but Ella was at the reception desk. "Hi, Ella," Anna greeted her. "Can you do me a favor? Tell Janice that I'll be out most of the day. I want to go over to Ben's for awhile."

"Sure thing, Anna," Ella said.

Anna waved and continued through the lobby out into the hot morning sun. The drive over to Ben's was made without the rag top of the Jeep. Anna let the wind blow through her hair, making it a wild mass of tangles when she finally pulled into Ben's drive. She pulled it into a rough braid, then hopped out of the car, dragging her camera and backpack with her.

The day was turning into a real steamer. Sweat rolled off her face and she tied a bandana around her neck, using it to brush at the moisture. Even at eleven the temperature was well above ninety, such a change from just a few days ago. She looked carefully around, then hid in some bushes to change into her bathing suit. The creek was looking better by the minute.

"Ah," she sighed, lowering herself into the cool water. She sat in the shallow water, letting it flow over her. "This is the life," she said, her quiet voice loud in the solitude of the forest. Birds sang in the trees overhead, but even they were worn from the heat. Anna stayed in the stream a bit longer, then reluctantly dragged herself out, wanting to take more pictures of the farm for the brochure she planned to do for Ben.

At two o'clock, Anna decided she had enough, and made her way back to the jeep. Although she had managed to push her upcoming meeting with Lance out of her mind while she was working, it came to the fore as soon as she reached the jeep. I'll just make sure Janice is around, she said to herself, praying that Lance would arrive while Janice was on duty at the desk.

Anna pulled into the parking lot of the hotel about three-thirty. She slipped out of the driver's seat, and walked into the lobby. The room, decorated with country accents, was quite pleasant under normal conditions, but Lance was standing in the middle of it, the proverbial steam coming out of his ears.

"Where have you been?" Lance demanded. He strode towards Anna, taking her arm in a firm grip. "I told you I wanted you to be here when I got here. I don't have time to play around. I've had to take a day away from shooting for this as it is." The more he spoke the tighter his fingers closed around her upper arm.

Anna was too stunned to speak for a minute, but when she finally found her voice, it was icy. "I don't remember asking you to come. In fact, I thought I made it perfectly clear that you weren't to come."

Lance's eyes narrowed at her tone. This was not what he had expected. Most women were cowed by his anger. It seemed to have the opposite effect on Anna. He would have to give this some thought, but not now. He was in a hurry. If he didn't have Anna back in Hollywood in two day's time, he would stand to lose a great deal of money, not to mention his hide, and if there was anything Lance valued it was his own skin.

A change of tactics was in order, Lance decided. He lowered his voice seductively and began to caress her skin with his fingers. "I missed you, honey. You weren't at home when I came back from my shoot, and I was worried."

Anna jerked her arm out of Lance's grip. "I hardly think so Lance," Anna scoffed. "Now that you know I'm safe," she said, stressing the word safe, "you are welcome to leave. I have things to do." She strode up the stairs, her back ramrod straight.

Lance stood at the bottom of the stairs, watching her ascent. This was going to be harder than he thought. He turned to the woman sitting at the desk. "Is it possible to get a room for the night?" he asked. If he could just spend some time alone with her, Anna might relent enough to come back with him. He had pegged her as a softie right from the beginning. If he could make her believe he was sorry for everything that had happened, he was certain she would come home with him.

"I'm sorry, but there aren't any rooms available," Janice, who had been watching the whole episode, informed him. "I could try to get you a room over in the next town if you'd like."

Lance was barely able to contain his frustration. "No thank you. I'll just share Anna's," he announced, then hurried up the stairs.

Janice was taken aback by his words. Knowing Anna the way she did, she was certain that the girl wouldn't 'share a room' with a man unless he was her husband. I hope she'll be all right, Janice thought, wishing she knew where Ben was staying.

Anna was sitting in front of the fireplace in her room when someone knocked on the door. She was just on her way to answer it when Lance's voice came through the panel.

"Anna, honey, let me in," he demand softly.

Anna hesitated, then reluctantly opened the door. She knew he would not go away until he had what he wanted, and thought it was best to find out exactly what it was before she threw him out. "What do you want, Lance?"

He pushed his way passed her, then turned and shut the door. He pulled her into his arms. "I knew you couldn't turn me away," he whispered in her ear.

Anna stood stiffly. I can't believe I actually thought I liked this guy, she thought. Who are you kidding, Anna Jenkins, a voice inside her said. You enjoyed all the attention you received when you were dating him. But I don't like being thought of as a plaything, she argued silently. And that's all he wants, someone to play with, and I've had enough of it.

Her voice, when she spoke to Lance, was dripping in sarcasm. "I managed to turn you away the last time we were together, Lance. And I suggest you let me go, or you will not be happy."

Lance let his arms fall, but he took her hands in his. "I apologized for that, Arianna. I was drunk. I know it was a foolish thing to do, and it won't happen again." He slid his hands up and down her arms. "I promise."

Anna looked Lance squarely in the eyes. "Lance, we are too different. I do not want the same things out of life as you do. I cannot live in your world, and I know that you don't like mine." She stepped away from his hands and went over to the window. "I'm not coming back to California," she announced.

A flash of anger went through Lance. So she's not coming back, is she? He'd see about that. But he would have to be careful. He only had a few days to get what he wanted. "Anna, don't make rash decisions. I promised I wouldn't act so thoughtlessly again. Just give us a few days together before you give me a final answer. I know I can make you happy." He joined her at the window. He turned her to face him, and tried to kiss her. Anna turned her head away. "Please Anna," he begged, trying another kiss. Anna again turned away.

"Don't try to kiss me, Lance," she demanded. "I don't want anything you're trying to sell."

This time Lance was not able to control the rage burning inside him. He grabbed her and forced his lips against hers. The arms surrounding her were bruising, as was the mouth covering hers. Anna struggled, which only incensed Lance. He pulled her towards the bed. Anna panicked. There was no way she could stop him if he intended to rape her, he was just too big. Her only chance was to break the hold he had on her. She slipped her foot between his legs and wrapped it around his calf. It was enough to throw him off balance. He let her go to save himself from falling, and Anna took the opportunity to put as much distance between the two of them as possible.

She ran over to the door and flung it open, racing down the hall towards the stairs. She didn't stop when Lance called to her, just kept running. Thank heaven I left my keys in my pocket, she thought, as she streaked passed a startled Janice McCray.

Janice only paused a moment, then came out from behind the desk, just as Lance reached the bottom of the stairs. She deftly stepped in front of him, stopping him in his tracks.

"I was able to get you a room at the Motor Inn in Wilburn," Janice told him, a false smile on her face.

"That's great," he said, trying to sidestep past her. He could see Anna making for the car park.

"You'll have to claim the room before six o'clock," she informed him.

"Fine, fine." He tried again to get past.

"That's in less than an hour," Janice went on as if nothing were amiss, hoping to give Anna more time to make her escape.

Anna had disappeared from view, but he saw her jeep passing the front window. "No problem,"Lance replied, forcefully moving Janice aside. He raced for his own car. He had to get to Anna. He couldn't afford for her to get away from him. Jumping inside his rented car, he ground the gears, and sped out of the drive, hot on Anna's tail.

Anna glanced nervously in her rearview mirror. Although she couldn't see anyone behind her, she was certain Lance would not give up his pursuit. She still hadn't figured out what he really wanted. His actions were strange and extremely aggressive, even for him. There had to be a reason behind his behavior, and knowing Lance, it couldn't be good. A voice inside her was telling her to run, and she had every intention of heeding it.

Her first thought was to run to Ben, but that was impossible. Even if she drove to Williamsburg, she had no idea where he was staying. And anyway, she didn't have enough gas to get there, and certainly didn't want to stop. Turning to look out the back window, Anna caught sight of her backpack. Her extra sleeping bag was also in the back. She had put it there yesterday, thinking she might spend some quiet time up in the mountains since Ben was going to be gone longer than anticipated. She had thought it would be a good time to gain some perspective on her life, but Lance's arrival was a much better reason to go into the mountains. He hated the outdoors, so she was fairly certain he wouldn't follow her. Even if he did try, his ability in the great outdoors was limited to finding the nearest hotel. There would be no way he could trail her if she got far enough into the park.

A second look in her mirror told her Lance was not as far behind as she would like. In fact, he was driving like a person possessed in his attempt to catch up with her. Anna drove steadily faster until she came to the state park entrance. She slowed her jeep enough to give a wave to the ranger in the park booth. He was not the same man who had been on duty when she and Ben brought the teens up earlier in the season.

"You're experienced?" he asked when Anna informed him of her intention to hike in the mountains. "I'd hate for something to happen out there." He gazed at her clothing in mild disbelief.

"Yes, I'm very experienced," Anna assured him with a tight smile. "I'm Arianna Jenkins."

The park ranger, familiar with her work, looked impressed. "Well, have a good time, Miss Jenkins. I hope to see some shots of our park in your next book."

Anna smiled again, a genuine one this time, despite the fear dwelling so near the surface. "You can count on it," she told him as she drove away. Looking back, she could see Lance sitting at the pull off, just before the entrance to the park. She grinned in triumph, feeling sure he wouldn't follow. Now her only problem would be how long to hide out before he lost interest in her.

At the park entrance Lance sat in his car, seething in anger. How had she gotten so far ahead of him? And what was he suppose to tell those men who were waiting for him and Anna to show up? He snapped his fingers, an idea coming to him. That was it. He carefully turned the car around and headed back to town. He needed to make a phone call.

Thirty minutes later, Lance was sitting in a road-side diner, his cellular phone at his ear. "I need some help," he told the person on the other end. "She got away ...Yes, I know I said I could handle her...She's somewhere in the Mountain State Park, here in Jordon...No, I can't go after her. I don't do nature. Look, if you want her, come and get her yourself. I found her for you, now the rest is up to you...Don't threaten me..." the conversation ended abruptly, making Lance extremely nervous. If Jack Jonson didn't get what he wanted from Anna, he would take it out of Lance without a qualm, and Lance had a low pain tolerance.

"Sorry, Arianna," he said softly. "But better you than me."

Seventeen

Ben couldn't shake the feeling that there was something terribly wrong. He did his best to concentrate on what was happening around him, since technically this was his meeting, but he kept glancing at his watch, wondering what it was that was bothering him so. He couldn't put his finger on it, but it was a familiar feeling, one he recognized as having before. He was so caught up in his thoughts he didn't hear Richard Weston speaking to him.

"Ben," the man said again. "What's the problem? You're miles away."

"I don't know, Richard. I keep getting this strange feeling that something is wrong, but I have no idea what."

Richard laughed. "It certainly isn't a problem with the board. They've approved every cent you asked for."

Ben gave an absent smile. "That's good," he said.

Richard shook his head. "You should be jumping for joy, Ben. You'll be able to open that youth retreat in the mountains by next spring."

Mountains. That word sent Ben back to when he and Arianna had taken the teens into the mountains for her photo shoot. He mentally snapped his fingers. That was it. The last time he had this feeling was then, when he couldn't shake the feeling that Arianna was in danger. That time it had been a bear in her path, but even after that incident the worry still nagged at him. Come to think of it, fear for her safety had plagued him even when she had been in West Virginia, rafting, and that was after he had informed her he wasn't planning on seeing her any more.

"Richard," Ben said, standing abruptly. "I have to go."

Richard was startled by the vehemence in Ben's voice. "Are you sure, Ben?"

Ben pulled on his sport coat as he answered. "Yes. One thing I've learned is to follow your instincts, and mine are screaming right now that there is something definitely wrong back in Jordon. I'm sorry to leave like this," he apologized.

"Don't worry about it Ben. There are only minor details left anyway, and I can sort those out for you as long as you leave your prospectus here. Go home and take care of whatever it is that's bothering you." Ben thrust the papers in Richard's hands and was out the door.

"Where's he going?" one of the bank board members asked.

Richard's gaze followed Ben. "He has to go back to Jordon. One thing about Ben. His instincts are the best. If he thinks there's something wrong at home, then there probably is." He turned to face the other men in the meeting. "Now, let's get back to the subject at hand."

Ben rushed down to the parking garage of the bank, taking the stairs instead of the elevator. Now that he was on his way, he felt the urge to hurry, as if being pushed from behind. He wished he had called Arianna before he left, but there had been no time. And he had left his cellular phone at the hotel. Not wanting to take the time to go back there, he headed the car straight to Jordon.

Anna stood next to her jeep in the gravel parking spot she had chosen. She took out the map of the park stuck in the glove box, and began mapping out her way. Not wanting to leave the park by the front entrance, she had no choice but to hike out and come pick up the jeep at a more convenient time, preferably when Lance was long gone. She studied the map carefully, noting that Ben's land was only a few miles away from the far western perimeter of the park. It would probably take her a day and a half, perhaps two, to hike that far considering she was at the most eastern point of the park at the moment, but that shouldn't be too much of a problem.

Her biggest concern was food. She folded the map carefully and stuck it in the pocket of her backpack. Opening the rear door of the jeep, Anna began rummaging through the boxes back there. "Thank you, God!" she whispered. Pulling open one of them, she found several packages of dried food, mostly trail mix, but also a couple of bags of dried noodles. That should last for awhile, Anna thought to herself, stuffing the packages into the main compartment of the backpack. Now I need something to heat the soup in.

In the last box she found an old tin cup, one she rarely used. This should work, she thought, putting it in with the food. There were a couple of candy bars in the glove box, Anna knew. She kept them there in case of emergencies, and she considered this one.

She rolled up the sleeping bag as tightly as she could, and tied it to the straps of the backpack. Anna hesitated over bringing her camera. Her natural inclination was to bring it with her, but it only added weight, and the pack she was using was not her usual heavy-duty hiking pack. She sadly put it back in the camera bag and slid it under the seat. Hopefully no one would break into the jeep before she was able to get back for it. This was her favorite camera and she didn't want to lose it. She secured the rag top tightly, and began her journey.

Starting off at a steady pace, Anna was able to make good time. The forest was peaceful, and her concerns about Lance's intentions momentarily faded into the background.

Lance, sitting in his hotel room in Wilburn was wondering about Anna. Although he cared for her in his own fashion, it wasn't enough to take the heat for the pictures she had in her possession. Unless he missed his guess, she didn't even realize she had taken pictures of one of the most elusive drug dealers in the country. But Jack Jonson knew she had, and wanted her and the pictures in his possession before the end of the week.

Lance's original plan had been to sweet talk Anna into returning to California. He thought he could do it over the phone, but when that failed he realized he would have to go to her and persuade her to return with him. Never having been refused by a woman, except for Anna, of course, Lance was not used to being thwarted, and it made him angry. Not to mention the fact that Jack was breathing down his neck, reminding him that if he didn't get Anna and the pictures, Lance would be in a great deal of pain. He had promised to spare Lance's life only if Lance delivered Anna to him personally. Jack had seen her at the party, her innocent beauty enchanting him, and at that moment had desired to possess her.

Guilt over his actions tried to force its way into Lance's consciousness, but he pushed it aside. She brought it all on herself, he defended himself. He had asked Anna to take pictures of him doing fun activities at that party, things he could use to promote himself. He never dreamed she would capture him making a drug deal. Foolish of him to be so careless, but he had really needed a fix. Once he realized what had happened it was too late. Anna had already left for Jordon. He didn't think he would have a problem getting Anna to come back to him. He had pegged Anna as the compliant type right away, although he had never been able to talk her into going to bed with him. That still rankled.

"Oh, well," he said aloud. "Jack will take care of that when he gets here." The man was due to arrive later this evening, to take matters into his own hands.

Unaware of the true danger she was in, Anna made camp early confident that Lance was not following her. The trail was proving harder than she had expected due to the heavy rain that had fallen last week. The air was hot and oppressive, making it difficult for Anna to breathe. Clouds were beginning to gather, and Anna knew she had to set up some type of shelter or she was going to get soaked. Not that being wet was her main concern. She was more worried about lightning, and being surrounded by trees she was a little of leery of getting hit.

Anna walked on for several minutes, finally finding a good start to her shelter among some fallen trees. There were enough branches laying around for her to lay them over the depression left beneath the trees, providing a make-shift roof. She dropped her backpack and sleeping bag into the shelter, then secured the branches with some twine she had in her pack. That done she hastily cleared an area to have a small fire. If rain was coming, this might be her last chance to get something warm inside her.

After eating her noodle soup, Anna doused the fire and went into her crude shelter. She curled up in her bag and was asleep in minutes.

Ben pulled into the parking lot of McCray House screeching to a halt before the gate that led to the patio. He rushed through, making his way straight to the kitchen where he knew Janice usually spent her evenings. She was fussing over the stove when he entered, startling her enough to make her drop the bottle of cleanser she was holding.

"Ben! You're going to give me a heart attack! What are you doing back?"

"Where's Arianna," he demanded, not answering her question.

Janice's eyes clouded. "I don't know. That Lance person was here earlier. I think he threatened her, Ben, or maybe worse. She went running out of here, and I thought she looked frightened."

"Where'd she go?"

"I don't know. I haven't seen her since then, and it's been hours since she left."

Ben ran his hand through his blond hair, making it stand almost on end. "What about Lance? Where'd he go?"

"I don't know that either. But I detained him as long as I could to give her time to get away from him." Janice paused for a minute. "I told him I didn't have room for him here, but I would get him a room in Wilburn. Maybe he went there," she added hopefully.

Ben hesitated. He was leery about driving out there and not finding the man. "Could you check and see if he's registered, Janice?"

"Sure," Janice agreed. Several minutes later she returned. "He has, but he's not there at the moment. It seems three other gentlemen joined him, and they left together about ten minutes ago."

Not sure how to approach the problem, Ben began pacing the kitchen tile. He could always go to Wilburn and wait for Lance to show up. That would probably be his best bet since Ben was certain that Lance was the key to finding Arianna.

"Janice, could you get some sandwiches and coffee together for me?" She looked at him in confusion. "I'm going to change then go to Wilburn and wait for Lance to get back to his room. Maybe I can convince him to help me." Ben's tone did not bode well for Lance, Janice could tell. Without a word she set about preparing his food. He thanked her then strode out to his truck, grateful that he had an extra pair of jeans and boots with him.

"Do you think something's happened to her, Ben?" Janice asked him when he returned to the kitchen. Worry lines were etched on her face.

"I just have this feeling, Janice. The same one I had a few weeks ago when we were up in the mountains." He took the food and ran out to his truck. Rain was beginning to fall, heavy drops that pounded against his windshield. He prayed that Arianna was safely tucked away in some hotel room, but couldn't shake the fear resting just below the surface.

When he pulled into the Motor Inn in Wilburn the rain was coming down in a steady stream. The receptionist readily gave him Lance's room number, telling him that Lance had returned alone a few minutes ago.

The knot in Ben's stomach tightened as he approached the room. Knocking on the door he waited impatiently, hearing shuffling footsteps on the other side.

Lance opened the door with savage energy. "I told you I won't go in there," he snarled, before registering Ben's presence. He tried hastily to shut the door when he realized his mistake, but Ben thrust his hand out, forcing the door all the way open.

"You can't do that," Lance complained. "Who are you, anyway?"

"Where's Arianna?" Ben demanded harshly.

Lance paled at the mention of her name. But he was determined not to incriminate himself. "I don't know what you're talking about," he hedged.

Ben's gaze seared Lance, who stepped back. Ben took hold of his arm, practically dragging the man farther into the hotel room. He kicked the door shut with his foot. "I want to know where she is," he demanded again, this time his voice cold.

Lance knew he was not going to be able to fool this giant standing in front of him. If he was lucky he could get rid of him, then make a run for it. Jack Jonson was certain to catch up with Anna before this guy, so Lance saw no reason to lie. "She's somewhere in the state park," he told Ben, jerking out of Ben's grasp.

Ben looked intently into Lance's eyes, and knew the man was telling him the truth, or at least part of it. Ben could tell Lance was holding something back, though. "What aren't you telling me?"

"I told you where she was. What else is there?" Ben just stood there, his very silence so intimidating that Lance was forced to admit, "There's someone else looking for her."

"Who?"

"Someone you don't want to mess with." Ben took a step towards him, and Lance hastily continued. "Jack Jonson. Name ring a bell?" When Ben shook his head, Lance sighed heavily. Guilt over what was going to happen to Anna was creeping into his consciousness despite his efforts to block it. "He's a big drug dealer from L.A."

Ben gasped. "What does he want with Arianna?"

"She took some pictures at a party we were attending. A few of them featured Jack making a drug sale. He wants them back, and he doesn't care what he does to get them."

"What exactly do you mean by that?" Ben asked, fear beginning to churn in his stomach.

"I mean that when he finds Anna, he'll take her, and no one will hear from her again."

Ben's face paled. He swore soundly, something he hadn't done since he was a rebellious teen-ager. He grabbed Lance in a grip of steel, dragging him out the door, totally ignoring Lance's protests. Throwing him into the truck, Ben harshly instructed Lance to buckle up, then sped out of the hotel parking lot. He drove straight to the Jordon police station, jumping out of the truck and rushing into the building.

Lance didn't move, knowing that right now there was no escape. When Ben came out, followed by several men, Lance sat there staring stonily ahead, wishing he had had more to drink. He made no effort to find out where they were going, he already knew. They were going to find Anna. Well, they may want to die, Lance thought, but that doesn't mean I have to go down with them.

When they reached the park entrance, Ben and the three policemen questioned the park ranger.

"Yes, Miss Jenkins went through about three or four, I guess."When asked what she planned to do, the ranger answered, "She said she was going to do some hiking. She didn't tell me where she was going, and seemed to be in a bit of a hurry. I figured she was working, so I didn't bother her with a lot of questions."

"Was there anything strange about how she looked?" Ben asked.

The ranger thought for a second. "Not strange really, although she wasn't exactly dressed for strenuous hiking, now that I think about it. And she kept looking over her shoulder, like she was nervous."

"Any other cars pull in tonight?" one policeman asked.

"Just one," he informed the man. "A Bronco came in with three guys in it. There was a car in the pull off, but I didn't pay much attention to it. It drove away when the Bronco went through. Is there a problem?"

Ben decided to confide in the ranger."Yes, there is. I have reason to believe that Miss Jenkins is in serious danger." He briefed the man on the details. "Any chance of getting a chopper up to make a search for her?"

The ranger was regretful. "Not in this weather. The storm is more severe than expected, so all aircraft have been grounded for the time being."

"Do you have any idea where she might have gone?" Ben asked again.

"Not really, but she took the western turn-off. When I made my rounds earlier this evening I saw her jeep parked in the west lot."

It wasn't much to go on but it was all they had. The four men stood in the office discussing their next move. When they moved out to Ben's truck it was to find the door open and the cab empty. Lance was no where to be seen.

"We'll get someone on it immediately, Ben," Jason White, police detective and friend, assured him. He called on the radio, informing the dispatcher about Lance's last whereabouts. "No doubt he's making a run for it. We want him in custody."

They drove to where Anna's jeep was parked, noting that the Bronco was also parked there. There was a marked trail, which Ben was sure Anna would take, at least to start. Janice had told him that Anna was wearing her cotton dress and a pair of tennis shoes when she ran out of the hotel that afternoon. It would be difficult to do any off trail hiking in that outfit.

"Let's go!" Ben shouted over the noise of the storm, which was growing steadily worse. Although the weather would impede their progress, Ben was grateful the other men looking for Anna would also have trouble.

✠✠✠✠✠

Anna awoke, startled. Something was urging her to move, and do it quickly. She peered out into the darkness, seeing nothing but the driving rain. She hesitated leaving her shelter, but the urge to run was growing by the second. Rather than ignore it, Anna gathered her things together, stuffing them into her back-pack. Her sleeping bag was hastily rolled, although she took the time to wrap it in it's plastic cover.

She stepped out into the night and was immediately pelted with stinging drops of rain. The wind whipped her hair every which way, making her aware that she hadn't pulled it up. Not wanting to take the time to mess with it, Anna hurried away from her shelter.

She was several yards away when she noticed the faint glow of a flashlight about a quarter of a mile beyond it. *Go quickly*, a voice inside her urged. Anna broke from the path and continued on until she was on a ridge overlooking the trail. From her vantage point, and with her eyes adjusted to the darkness, she could vaguely see her impromptu camp. The light was there, and Anna caught voices floating on the wind.

"She's not here," one voice said.

Another sarcastically answered. "No kidding. Lance said she was an outdoors woman, but I doubt she could go far in this storm. Come on."

Anna started at the mention of Lance. These men knew him, which didn't bode well for her. Somehow she knew these men were the reason behind Lance's strange behavior. Anna also knew that she had to hurry. She wouldn't be able to rely on outside help to get her out of here. Her only hope was to get to Ben's.

She turned to leave, but the rain had slickened the slope, and her feet slid out from beneath her. Her involuntary yelp of fear was loud enough to be heard in the lull of the storm. The flashlight whipped around, exposing her in the night.

"There she is!" one man cried. They rushed in her direction.

Anna dragged herself up, using branches to get her balance. She was still some distance away from her followers, but if she didn't get a move on they would catch up with her quickly. Instead of winding her way around the slope she was on, Anna decided they best way to get from point A to point B was a straight line. She was experienced enough to climb in the dark,but the rain, again falling in earnest, not to mention the fact she was wearing a dress and tennis shoes, was bound to cause a problem.

Dropping her pack and sleeping bag, Anna began her ascent, hoping the men trailing her wouldn't have any climbing experience. She picked her way carefully, digging toe holds with her fingers. The rain was making the slope extremely hazardous, but when she looked down and saw the men almost to her starting point, she ignored the danger and plunged ahead.

Eighteen

Ben and the three officers came upon Anna's deserted camp forty minutes later. There was no sign of her, but one of the men noticed the abundance of footprints.

"They found it, too," he stated. He looked at Ben, waiting for his decision on what to do next.

Rain dripped down Ben's back as he stood contemplating their next move. His instincts were telling him to move on, that Anna was still free for the moment. He told the others as much, and they pushed on, following the tracks still visible in the mud. They came to the place where Anna had left the trail. Ben stopped suddenly as a thought occurred to him. Anna was headed west, now taking a direct path in that direction. The back of his land butted up against the state property, on the far western border of it. Could Anna possibly be making for his house?

"Jason, I think I know where's she going," Ben exclaimed. He told the officer his theory.

"That's possible, Ben." Jason spoke into his walkie-talkie. "Get someone out to Ben's place," he told the dispatcher. "We have reason to believe Anna's headed in that direction. Get some men and have them start east from there," he added. He looked at Ben. "We'll find her, Ben."

"I just hope it's before they do," Ben said grimly.

Anna was always conscious of the men behind her. They weren't closing in on her, but she wasn't gaining any ground either.It seemed as if the wind and rain were working against her. As she struggled against the elements, Anna prayed, knowing the Lord was the only help she had.

Just when she thought she might be making some headway, Anna's foot slipped into a deep hole, and she twisted her ankle sharply. The pain was so severe she cried out in agony. She gripped it tightly, hoping to stop the pain shooting up her leg. Over the sound of the storm she could hear the men making their way through the brush behind her. There was no time to waste. She took the bandana from around her neck and tied it tightly around her ankle praying it would enable her to keep walking.

It did, but just barely. Anna was thankful the bone wasn't broken, but the injury slowed her progress considerably. She picked up a large branch, and used it for a walking stick. She had given up trying to estimate where she was. Looking at the illuminated dial of her watch, she noticed it was well past midnight. She guessed she had walked about ten miles, give or take, since she set off earlier in the evening.

The rain didn't show any indication that it was going to stop any time soon. With any luck it would hinder the men following her as much as it was her. They now had the advantage over her. She couldn't walk as fast as she had been. But she still had her skill, and since these were acquaintances of Lance's it was more than likely that they weren't fans of the great outdoors.

Anna mentally reviewed the map. If she remembered correctly, she was at the highest point in this part of the park. She peered through the rain, trying to decide which way to go. If she was where she thought she was, Ben's property was about four miles to her right. The way was rough, with no trail to speak of, and the rain was making the ground treacherous. She would be going downhill, which was a blessing, but there was also the possibility of mud slides. The ground was saturated with water, and more was falling from the sky every minute. She would have to risk it, praying the Lord would guide her.

Ben was praying as well, that the Lord would lead Anna to safety. Several times he and the officers had spotted a light in the darkness ahead. Anna, Ben surmised, wouldn't have a flashlight with her. He remembered her telling him she had lost it on the rafting trip. Moreover, they had found Anna's pack discarded at the bottom of a steep slope. That only left Jonson and his men.

"Think they have her?" Jason asked Ben when they stopped to catch their breaths.

"No, I don't think so," Ben answered. "If they did, they'd head back this way. They probably have no idea where they're going, They're just following Arianna." Ben bent down, resting his hands on his knees. He was tired, and if he was he knew that Arianna had to be more so.

Suddenly his glance was caught by something shiny. He reached down, and grasped the chain in his hand. Arianna's gold ankle chain. He crouched down, investigating the area. There were broken branches around, the chain resting on one that was at the top of a deep hole. The rain had washed away most traces, but Ben was certain that Anna had fallen in the hole. Her chain must have caught on the branch when she pulled her leg out of the hole.

"I think she's hurt," Ben said suddenly. "We have to get moving." With that the men quickened their pace.

Not far ahead of them, Jack Jonson was swearing up a storm to rival the one crashing around him. He had thought it would be an easy task to find the girl and haul her back to California. But she was proving to be a worthy opponent. Most women he knew could barely walk on level ground let alone trudge through the wilderness in the mud. He knew she knew she was being followed, and was leading him a merry chase. She was also much more experienced than Jack had given her credit for. Despite that, he had to get her. Those pictures were much too incriminating to have around. Even if she didn't realize what they were, it wouldn't take long for someone to make the connection. Once he had her taken care of, he would take care of Lance. The man was a thorn in Jack's side, and Jack didn't like thorns.

He trudged on in the rain, head bent against the wind. He noticed, not for the first time, that the girl seemed to be dragging her right foot. Back a ways he had seen a hole. She must have fallen in it. Lifting his head he urged his men to hurry. "She's slowing down. We should be able to catch her soon."

Anna knew she was in trouble. The downward slope was hard on her ankle, and she was having difficulty keeping her balance in the slippery mud. She could sense the men behind her, closer now. Their light hit the ground in back of her. Another sweep and she would be caught in the beam.

She picked up her pace as much as she could. But in her hurry she slipped, sending mud sliding down ahead of her. Unable to catch herself, she was swept downhill in a cascade of flowing mud. She bounced off hidden rocks and careened off small trees, until she landed in a heap at the bottom of the hill. Dazed, she looked upwards, staring into the beam of the flashlight.

"There she is!" one man yelled. They didn't want to slide downhill as well, so they picked their way cautiously down the slope. When they finally reached the bottom Anna was nowhere to be found.

"Where'd she go?" Jack yelled. Just then a tremendous flash of lightning illuminated the whole area. Jack could see Anna limping through the field ahead of him. "There," he shouted. He ran, followed by his two companions.

Anna glanced back in fear. They were too close. There was no way she could outrun them. The flash of lightning had momentarily brightened the area, and Anna saw the river, swollen from the heavy rains. If she could get to it, there was a good chance she could get away, if she didn't drown first. Knowing she had no choice, Anna headed straight for the raging waters.

"If she gets to the water, we'll never catch her," Jack screamed. He sprinted the last remaining yards between him and Anna, but was too late. Just as he reached out to grab her, she jumped into the river.

Anna knew she was in serious trouble the minute she hit the water.It pulled at her, trying to suck her down into its depths. Anna fought it, struggling to get to the opposite shore, but it kept pushing her back to where Jack was waiting. She went down under the water and came up sputtering. Again and again the river forced her beneath, until finally she could fight it no longer. She washed up on shore a few feet from where Jack was standing.

He hauled the unconscious woman up the bank. She was still alive, and he grinned maliciously. He was going to take great pleasure in punishing her for the merry chase she had led him on.

"Ralph, get over here," he called over the storm. When the man appeared he said, "Toss her over you shoulder."The man hefted her up, and none to gently threw her over his shoulder. He had just turned to start the journey back, when the other man shouted a warning.

"Someone's coming," he panted, running to met Jack and Ralph.

Jack thought fast. He was positive whoever was coming was after the girl. Should he try to make a run for it, toting her as well, and take the chance of getting caught? Or should he dump her in the river, waiving the punishment he so wanted to give her? Then he struck on a plan. He would let whoever it was find her. Then he would follow them to wherever, and retrieve the girl another time.

"Dump her!" Jack hissed. He beckoned the men to follow him, and they melted into the forest.

"Arianna!" Ben called frantically. They were almost to the river, and had lost sight of the light they had been following. "Arianna!"

The four men swept the area with their flashlights. There, a short way ahead, lay a body, almost impossible to see in the long grass. "Anna!" Ben cried, rushing to her. He lifted her up in his arms, cradling her against his chest. She was still breathing, much to Ben's relief.

Jason handed Ben a blanket from his pack. "Here, wrap her in this." Working together, the managed to get Anna wrapped in the blanket.

"I've called the station to let them know we've found

her," Ron informed Ben and Jason. "But there's trouble. A tornado was spotted about thirty miles west of here, coming this way. If we don't find some shelter soon, we'll get caught."

Ben looked at the river. "This is the river that runs at the back of my property. My creek is an off branch of it. My house is only a few miles beyond here."

"But how do we get across the river?"Jason asked, eyeing the raging waters.

"There's a bridge about half a mile that way," Ben said, point to his left.

"Let's get going!"

The four men trudged through the mud and rain, unaware of the danger behind them. They reached the bridge, and gingerly crossed it. The water below was crashing against the pilings, making the bridge sway dangerously. Ben held the still unconscious Anna tightly against him, letting Jason guide him as he crossed.

Jack and his men waited until Ben and the rest were just out of sight, then they crossed the bridge as well. "We can overtake them on this side. The guy said his house isn't too far away. We can get the girl, get to the house, and be on our way from there."

The men were very eager tofinish this assignment.The rain was cold, and coming down harder. With any luck they would be able to overcome the four men and get the girl with a minimum of fuss. They steadily crept up on Ben and the others, until finally they were in position to strike.

Ron, bringing up the rear, went down in a heap when Ralph smashed him in the back of the head with a rock. The storm masked any sounds that were made, leaving the other three unaware of any problem. Todd fell next. Jason and Ben, who were quite a distance ahead of the other two didn't immediately notice their missing comrades.

Ben stopped abruptly. He had the strangest feeling they were being followed. He turned around, and was almost flattened by Ralph's fist. He managed to dodge in time, but lost his balance and fell. Jason heard the commotion and rushed back to help his friend. Ben rolled away from Anna and jumped to his feet. Ralph's companion joined in the fray.

The two large men were too much for Jason and Ben. Ben's last conscious thought was a prayer for Anna's safety.

Ralph limped over to where Anna lay, and picking her up, threw her once again over his shoulder. "Let's go," he commanded the other man. They met Jack, who took the lead once again.

"That guy said his house was a few miles west. We'll head due west from here," he commanded, taking a compass out of his pocket. "That way."

The wind had picked up considerably, making walking difficult. The jarring of her head against Ralph's back brought Anna back to consciousness. She moaned slightly, but it went unheeded in the noise of the storm. She was having trouble thinking clearly, her head ached so badly. She had no idea where she was or why she was being carried this way. Certainly Ben would never treat her in this manner.

Then it hit her. This wasn't Ben. These were Lance's friends, or whatever Lance called them. They must have found her. But she had a dim recollection of being in Ben's arms earlier. What if they had hurt Ben? Anna couldn't bear to think about it.

"Up ahead!" Jack yelled, his voice barely audible over the noise of the wind. Anna turned her head slightly and could see a light through the rain. Ben's house? she wondered foggily. If it were she might be able to get help.

The constant jarring of her head made Anna nauseous. She began to fade in and out of consciousness, until finally everything was black.

Nineteen

Ben came to with a start, water beating on his face. He rolled over to see Jason just beginning to rise. "We've got to find them!" Ben cried weakly. His head felt like an elephant had walked over it, and his body felt bruised and battered. By the looks of things Jason wasn't much better off. Knowing they couldn't leave the other two out in the weather, they backtracked and found them leaning up against a tree.

"Don't worry about us," Ron said. "We'll follow as soon as we can."

Ben took them at their word, and he and Jason fought their way through the wind towards Ben's house. "The wind's picking up even more," Jason yelled. Indeed, it was screeching through the trees.

"That tornado must be close. We've got to hurry." Ben's watch told him that Jonson had a fifteen minute head start. Good thing I know all the short-cuts, Ben thought. He led Jason through the woods, instead of going through the field. "This will bring us to the house on the opposite side of Jonson, as long as he went through the field," Ben called to Jason. Although it was still blowing, the wind was less harsh in the protection of the trees.

"Hopefully they'll have enough sense to stay at the house," Ben said. "They probably think there's no threat from us. Maybe we can use that to our advantage."

"What do you have in mind?" Jason wanted to know.

"I don't really know. It would be better for us if we can get to each man separately."Ben was silent, thinking. "I just don't see how we can do it."

"They won't be expecting us. We have the element of surprise on our side," Jason told him. "We'll have to take advantage of it." They bandied around a few ideas until they decided on a plan.

"Remember when we were kids?" Jason asked Ben suddenly.

Ben looked surprised. "Yeah, what about it?"

"It's just like the time we snuck into Mr. Rylies' barn. He was in there, so instead of going in the back, like he thought we would, we went in the front."

"So what?"

"Jonson will probably keep the front and back door covered. But what about the cellar?"

A light went on in Ben's head. There was a separate entrance to the house through the cellar. Ben had discovered it not too long ago. It had been boarded up, and not used for so long no one remembered it was there, except for Jason of course. "If we can get it open without making too much noise, we should be O.K. The storm will mask most of it."

They reached the edge of the woods, and could plainly see the house. The rain had slowed to a steady stream, but the wind was whipping fiercely. Branches flew, spiraling around the barn. "It's coming," Jason stated flatly. He had lived through one of the worst tornadoes to hit the area, and Ben trusted his judgment.

"How long?" Ben asked.

Jason stepped out of the protection of the trees for a moment. "Maybe twenty minutes," he said, coming back. "It's going to be a hum-dinger, too."

Ben gripped his friend's hand. "Let's pray before we go, Jase." The two men bowed their heads. "Lord," Ben said. "We ask that you help us in what we're trying to accomplish. Grant us your speed and protection that we can free Arianna. Keep us safe from the approaching storm, and from physical harm. In your name, Amen."

As stealthily as they could, Ben and Jason approached the house. Ben could see a light in the kitchen window, but no one was visible. A good sign, he thought, as they came up to the back porch. The cellar door was just under the window, and Ben knew they would have to work quickly. Without too much fuss the door was forced open and the two men descended the stairs.

"O.K. We're in. Now what?" Jason whispered.

"How should I know? You're the policeman. Think of something," Ben hissed back. He listened carefully. The wind was howling, beginning to get a queer whistling sound to it. "But hurry. We're running out of time."

Jason moved past Ben towards the door that led to the rest of the house. "The kitchen was empty when we got in here. Hopefully it still will be." Both men crept up the stairs, as quietly as possible.

Crouching by the door, Ben whispered, "They're probably in the living room. It gives the best view of the west. If they're watching the weather, that's where they should be." He turned to peer at Jason in the dim light coming from underneath the door. "Go back down and get that shovel hanging by the furnace." Jason moved back down the stairs and returned with the shovel, as well as a sledge hammer.

"This was laying on the floor by the shovel," he said to Ben. "Been working off some steam?"

"Funny," Ben shot back. He cautiously opened the door, and looked around. No one around, he signaled to Jason. They stepped out into the hall, and warily peered around the corner of the kitchen door. The three men stood around the front window gazing anxiously at the debris blowing around the front yard. Anna lay on the couch, apparently unconscious.

Jason pointed to the man on the right, miming that he would take care of him, which left the other two for Ben. Jason couldn't tell if they were armed, but Ben caught his warning glance. He held up three fingers, then two, then one. When the last one went down the two rushed into the room.

Ben threw himself at the man farthest left. The momentum sent them sailing through the front window, sending glass in all directions. Ben landed on top of the man, knocking the wind out of him, rendering him unconscious. When he was sure the man was out, Ben clambered back through the broken window. The other man, still in shock over the suddenness of the attack, was not nearly as large, and Ben was able to easily subdue him. Jason, too, handled his opponent without difficulty. He pulled out two pairs of handcuffs and slipped them over the men's wrists.

Wind shrieked through the shattered window. "We've got to get out of here," Jason cried over the noise.

Ben peered out into the darkness. The man who had fallen through the window was still unconscious. "I'll get him. You take the other two downstairs." He glanced over at Anna. She was safe enough for the moment.

Jason dragged his captives through the room and down the stairs. He cuffed them to the stair railing, and went up to help Ben. "Hurry!" he shouted. The wind had increased even more, and the predawn sky was an inky green color. "It's coming!" He took the man from Ben leaving him to go after Anna.

Ben threw the quilt that lay on the back of the couch over Anna and picked her up. Holding her close, he struggled against the wind through the kitchen and into the basement. After the noise of the storm, the cellar was eerily quiet, except for one man trying to talk Jason into letting them go.

"Sure, I'll let you go right now. Feel free. We'll pick you up when the tornado decides to drop you," he retorted sarcastically.

"How long, Jase?" Ben asked, referring to the length of time they would be stuck underground.

Jason listened for a moment."It's moving fast. It shouldn't be more than fifteen minutes." He looked over at the three men attached securely to the stair rail. "Get comfy. You'll be here a little longer than that."

Ben sat against the far wall, cuddling Anna in his arms. Jason joined him. "How is she?" he asked.

Looking down at her, he noticed how pale she seemed. "I

don't know," Ben replied. "I've got to get her into town. Doc Watson needs to take a look."

Just then Anna stirred. Moaning, she opened her eyes a slit. When her eyes lighted on Ben, she gave a contented sigh and closed her eyes again.

"That's encouraging Ben," Jason teased. "She sees you and passes right out. You must be a really exciting date."

"Well, at least I have one," Ben retorted.

"What do you mean?" Jason feigned surprise. "I have three right over there." He pointed to the men huddled by the stairs.

"Yeah, but mine's prettier."

They sat listening to the storm for twenty more minutes, then Jason went upstairs to see what was going on. He moved through the living room, noting that other than the front window, there was very little damage except a very wet carpet. When he reached the front door, he threw it open. The sun was just beginning to peek out from behind the fast moving clouds. Just as he turned to yell down to Ben, a police squad car came squealing into the drive.

"Hey guys," he called to the officers exiting the car."What took you so long?"

"We took the scenic route," one of them called back. "We thought Ron and Todd might like to get back home, instead of playing Rambo with you and Ben."

"Were they all right?" Jason asked, his tone serious. Ron and Todd were great guys, two of his finest officers, and he didn't want to hear that they had been seriously hurt.

"They're fine. Ron has a slight concussion, Todd a broken wrist. Other than that, everything is great."

Jason led the men into the house. "I have a present for you," he told them. "It's clear, Ben!"

Ben came up the stairs, Anna still held close. "Hi guys," he greeted the other officers. "You're a little late."

"So Jason tells us."

"I'll leave you to finish up here, Jason. I need to get Anna to the hospital," Ben said.

"You need a ride?" one officer asked.

Ben shook his head. "No. I've got a car here." Two of the officers followed Ben out to the barn where Ben had stored the car he had borrowed for his grandparent's upcoming visit, and helped him get Anna settled in the back seat.

"Hope she's all right, Ben," they said as he drove away. He gave them a wave, and pulled out into the road.

It was a difficult trip. Trees were down everywhere, evidence that the tornado had indeed ripped through the area. But miraculously, there were no roadblocks to delay getting Anna to the hospital.

"How is she, Doc?" Ben questioned the man when he came into the waiting room. Ben had been sitting there for over an hour, after being informed that Doc needed to examine Anna thoroughly.

Doc frowned. "She seems to be fine, Ben. But she took in a lot of water, so we'll have to keep an eye on her overnight. She hasn't regained consciousness yet, and that worries me."

"Can I see her?"

"Not right now. I want her to stay isolated for a bit. Plus you're needed elsewhere. Janice called me. She and Ella could use some help at the hotel."

Ben left with reluctance. He hated to go, but knew he wasn't doing anyone any good moping around the hospital. Helping the town clean up after the storm would take his mind off the worry. He hoped.

There was quite a bit of damage in town. McCray House had lost a couple of trees. Thankfully none had fallen on the roof, although one had landed on Janice's car. Downtown had gotten off lightly as well. Signs were down, as well as some of the smaller trees, but the only real damage was blown in windows. People milled around the square, wondering what to do first. Quite a few of them were video taping the scene to help with insurance. Ben lent a hand, and the clean up began.

It was several hours later when Ben returned to the hospital. He had stopped by the florist and picked out a bouquet of roses for Arianna. Red and white, to tell her how much he loved and cherished her. She was sitting up in bed when he entered.

Without pause he went directly to her and kissed her for all he was worth. She responded, but then he felt her shaking, and he pulled away thinking he was hurting her. Instead her found her doing her best not to break out in giggles.

"What's so funny, woman?" he demanded, feeling slightly put out.

"I'm sorry, love. I didn't mean to laugh," Anna tried to sooth his ruffled feelings. She looked coyly through her long lashes. "And just to put the record straight, I don't find you boring in any way."

Ben was startled. "You heard that?"

"Oh yes. I think I started coming to when you picked me up. The arms were different than the man who had me before.But my head hurt so much it was hard to open my eyes. Then I heard your voice, and I just had to find out if it was a dream." She reached up a hand to touch his cheek. "I prayed so hard that you would come for me."

He grasped her hand, and pressed it harder onto his face. "I couldn't shake the feeling that there was something wrong. I hightailed it back to Jordon, and found out that Lance had been to see you, and you hadn't been seen since."

Anna shuddered. She had almost forgotten Lance. "I was so scared. He acted so strange. He followed me to the park, but I knew he wouldn't go in. Who were those men chasing me?" she wanted to know.

Ben hesitated. "They were drug dealers, Arianna."

"What!?" Her face turned pale. "Lance was messing with drug dealers?"

"It seems that way. You inadvertently took some pictures

of them at a party. The man wanted them back, and you as well."

Anna reached for Ben, who willingly pulled her close. "They're in custody, sweetheart. They can't hurt you," he tried to reassure her.

Still, it was frightening to think that a drug dealer had been pursuing her and she hadn't even known the real danger she was in. If he had gotten away, it was possible she may never have been seen again. Reaction set in, and she began to tremble.

Ben tightened his hold, running his hand down her hair, calming her. "It's all right now, sweetheart," he whispered.

Just then the door burst open, and Jason came strolling in. "Hi, Ben! How's tricks?"

Ben glared at him. Jason always did have an awful sense of timing.

Knowing what Ben was thinking, Jason grinned. "I just wanted to tell you my news. Those men are wanted big time in L.A. The F.B.I. out of Williamsburg helicoptered in just a little while ago, and took them into custody." He looked over to Anna. "They want to talk to you, but they said there was no hurry. It seems they have enough evidence to put them away for quite awhile, even without the little kidnaping sideline."

Ben got up and shook Jason's hand. "Thanks for the help, Jase."

The man grinned broadly. "Just make sure I get an invite to the wedding. And you might think about naming your first child after me."

Anna blushed furiously, but Ben just laughed. "We're going to have a girl first. And I don't plan on naming her Jasonette." He pushed Jason out of the room and shut the door behind him.

Turning back to Anna, he took her hands in his. "I didn't plan on doing it this way. I wanted to show you how romantic I can be. But I can't wait, Arianna. Will you marry me?" He went down on one knee, then groaned. He had forgotten the bruises.

Tears flowed slowly down Anna's cheeks. But they were

happy tears. She loved this man so much, had prayed so hard that the Lord would let them be together, and now it was all coming true. “I’ll marry you,” she whispered. Ben stood, and Anna raised her face for the kiss she knew was coming.

Twenty

"Do I look all right?" Anna's voice was higher pitched than normal, and Lauren laughed.

"Relax, Arianna. You look beautiful." Which was not quite the truth. In actual fact, Anna was breathtaking. Her white satin dress flowed around her like a cloud, a shaft of sunlight making the pearls sewn into the bodice gleam. The off the shoulder neckline left her shoulders bare, the white of the dress setting off her golden tan. Ben had asked that she leave her hair long and uncovered, so Lauren had taken hair on either side and braided it, weaving tiny sprigs of baby's breath throughout. She clasped them at the back of Anna's head with a barrette, then added small white roses and more baby's breath.

She stood back and studied the picture Arianna made. It was indeed beautiful, and Lauren couldn't help feeling a little envious of her friend. For years she had been praying for a special man to enter her life, but so far the Lord had been silent. She shook her head to rid herself of the melancholy thoughts. This was her friend's wedding day, and after all that Arianna had been through in her life, Lauren was thankful that she had found someone as special as Ben.

"It's time to go, Arianna," Lauren gently prodded her. "Ben's grandfather will be waiting at the bottom of the stairs."

Ben and Arianna had decided to marry at McCray House, having the ceremony in the gardens behind the house. Janice had been ecstatic when she was told and had truly outdone herself. She had set up an arch at the back of the garden, and had woven roses and ivy all through it. Chairs were set up, covering almost the entire area, leaving only an aisle for Anna to walk down.

Ben was standing impatiently in front of the arbor, Jason at his side, grinning at his friend's discomfiture. No way was he ever going to go through this, Jason assured himself. Too much trouble. The music changed, signaling that Anna was about to make her appearance. Jason turned to watch, and his eyes widened at the vision coming down the aisle.

She was tall, probably not much shorter than he was, and her forest green dress set off her sun-bleached blonde hair. Bright blue eyes returned his stare before she turned to the opposite side. As she stood opposite him, Jason was hard pressed to do his best man duties.

Ben took his eyes off the aisle for a moment to grin at Jason's lack of attention. Lauren was a beauty, for sure. But then he caught sight of Arianna, standing at the patio door, his grandfather at her side, and all thoughts of Jason and Lauren were wiped from his mind. Never had he seen this woman look so incredibly breathtaking. He was almost blinded by her beauty.

As she walked down the aisle, Ben lifted his heart in a brief prayer of thanksgiving. When he opened his eyes, they met Arianna's. She was smiling, her beautiful, dark brown eyes misty. Ben felt tears sting his own eyes. This woman was going to be his for the rest of their lives.

Anna smiled as she met Ben's eyes. The gray eyes were no longer somber as they had been on the day they had first met. So much had changed for both of them in the months since then. She and Ben had each come to terms with the promises they had made, and instead of feeling bound by them, they felt free. Free to live the lives God intended them to live.

With each other.